Published by Honno
'Ailsa Craig', Heol y Cawl, Dinas Powys
South Glamorgan, Wales, CF64 4AH

1 2 3 4 5 6 7 8 9 10

The author would like to stress that this is a work of fiction and no resemblance to any actual individual or institution is intended or implied.

ISBN 978 1 90678403 4

Published with the financial assistance of the Welsh Books Council

Cover image: Ed Freeman, © Getty Images
Cover design: G. Preston

Printed in Wales by Gomer

Flint

by

Margaret Redfern

HONNO MODERN FICTION

To my sons, David and Matthew; and to Robert Evans,
'Music Man'

One

Huddle into yourself. Heft the blanket round you. Ice cracks in its folds, settles into silence. Frost ghosts the marsh grass. Nightjars are noiseless. Dark rises up from the land. It swallows the sky. No moon: it is neap tide. The sea is hussing behind the sea bank, safe, caged. Wind shivers hard reeds. They rattle like bones. Far off, a screech owl on the hunt. Black pools glitter with stars. The real stars are high above. They are singing inaudibly, endlessly, in the cosmos that stretches to infinity over the flat fens. Tonight, if you listen hard. Tonight, if you are patient. Huddle inside your whitening shroud. Settle yourself to wait.

Two months after they showed off the Welsh prince's head through the streets of London, my brother Ned sent me a token that told me I'd never see him again. I'd seen neither hide nor hair of him since we'd said our goodbyes one bleak morning of dismal rain. Now, four years almost to the day, here was Ralf back from the Welsh war with the stench of blood on him still. He'd come to give me the swan pipe, the pipe Ned always kept with him, ever since the day he was given the swan's wing and told that the birds were fallen angels. Well, tell Ned that and he wasn't going to rest until he turned that wing into a pipe. The sound of it was aching sweet. Don't know if it was the voice of an angel – I never heard one – don't think it sounded much like a swan, either. It was Ned's soul that sang.

Not a doubt it was Ned's pipe. I recognised the marks on it. I knew how they got there.

'Ned gave it to me,' he said. 'It's for you. I'm sure he meant the pipe is for you.'

He must have seen how I felt. The words were falling out of his mouth.

'Listen, Will,' he said, 'if they find out I've done this, they'll do for me for sure. They say he turned traitor. They were looking for him and that red-headed friend of his. Don't tell nobody you've seen me, Will. I've my wife and bairns to think of.'

I promised I wouldn't but I wasn't thinking about him, nor his wife and brats.

'How was he?' I asked. I sounded flat calm but I could barely get the words out, my jaw was that stiff. I could hardly breathe and my head was bursting. What I meant was, is he still alive? Or – God help him – taken? Better off dead than Edward's prisoner—

'He was just the same.' Ralf looked amazed, as if he'd expected Ned to grow horns and a tail. 'I knew him straight off, in spite of the robes. He was wearing the robes of the white monks. He'd a shaved bone house an' all.' He stopped. His eyes flickered away from mine and his voice wasn't steady anymore. 'Alive, Will, but after? I don't know. I didn't see him. We'd been given the order to go in and take the place. So that's what we did. I didn't lay a finger on him, Will, I swear to God. Don't blame me.'

I didn't. That's what happens in war. Nobody and nowhere is sacred.

Maybe he'd got away. Miracles did happen. People talked about them happening. The priests told us about them. There was the story about the dead man coming alive again because Our Lord made it so. And the holy woman who had her head chopped off and then the saint put it back on her neck, all right and tight. Not like the poor, slaughtered prince. His head was up there on a spike on London's walls. Maybe that was what had happened to Ned.

Odd, this parleying with the enemy. Odd, too, that Ralf was the enemy when we'd grown up together. And Ned parting with the pipe; that was the oddest thing of all. He loved that pipe. That's why I knew he was gone for good. And I wished again, as I'd done every day, every hour, for four whole years, that I'd never left him. I wanted to howl but I didn't. What was the point? We'd made our choices four years back and there was no changing things now. I looked at it; a small length of yellowed bone, not even as big as my hand span, with a few holes bored in. Nothing much to look at. I tried to blow into it but there was nothing, no sound, except for the hiss of breath between my teeth. I knew it wouldn't sing for me. It needed Ned to do that. Without him, there was no song. I squeezed back the sorrow that choked my throat. Ralf deserved a welcome.

'Come and eat with us. Stay the night. The wind's rising and by the look of those clouds there's a rare storm on the way. It won't be safe to cross the fen.'

'It's not safe here, Will. I'd best be on my way. I can make Boston before dark. If they knew I'd come to find you – I can't risk it.'

We clasped hands. We were friends once, before the wars. Then Ralf was gone, striding out along the fen path. I never did know what happened to him. He didn't deserve to die, even if he had the blood of God's men on his hands. But that was the night of the great gale when the sea covered the land and killed so many. Boston was hit hard. The abbey at Spalding was wrecked and many churches where folk took shelter, poor devils. Our whole world was in danger. I saw my mother and sisters swept away in front of my eyes, and I couldn't do a thing to stop it happening. Why was I left to linger? I've asked myself that many a time. Maybe God knew it was more punishment for me to live than to die. Or maybe He offered me the chance of redemption. See. I've learned long words, living here.

That day, long after Ralf was lost to sight along the fen track, I gripped Ned's swan pipe tight in my hand and I could see him plain as if he was standing in front of me: tall, thin, gawky, with bright black eyes in a bony face and a thatch of black hair. When he walked, it was sideways on, like a crab, a bit bent over. His hand kept coming up to push the hair off his face or he'd scratch his eyebrow or the back of his neck with bony fingers. Once, he forgot about the knife he was holding and the point just missed his eye. He didn't even know. We didn't look like brothers. In those days, I was a mouth on short, skinny legs, spouting like a gargoyle in a rainstorm, always ready with a tale to tell to get us out of the mire Ned landed us in. Not that he meant to.

I've told a bagful of stories in my time; some of them downright lies. Folk are ready and willing to believe anything, if you tell it right. I've made enough out of it to keep me snug in my old age. But this one, this story, there's not one word of it a lie and not one word of it spoken until today. Still, you've only got my word for that, haven't you? And what are words, when all's said and done? Where do they get us, in the end? Ned didn't need words. He had his own way of talking.

For four years, I kept a hope. But that day I knew he'd never be back and I'd never see him again. Well, there it is. All washed away, you might say.

Can't do any harm, now, to tell this story.

But where do I start? Wait. I'll build up the fire. There'll be frost tonight. And these rooms might be built out of good stone but they're cold. Like a tomb. My bones ache in winter.

That summer's journey. That will do well on a night like this. If I cross back and forth and in and out, bear with me. This story's as full of twists as those carvings you see on the old crosses.

Listen.

It was that hot, dry summer of '77. Out of the thirty of us, only two were glad to be leaving – three, if you count me. The rest were glum. They didn't want to go to war, and not at Lammas. But Peter Long was nabbed one night with at least two sticks of eels filched from the Abbot's own fishery. Not an easy matter, hiding fifty writhing eels. Besides, the Abbot's men were on the watch for him. It meant a heavy punishment, so for him this journey was deliverance as miraculous as his namesake's. Or so he said. Long words and long winded, that was Peter. Long everything, so he said. Small wonder we called him Peter Long. He liked it. Called it his creed. He'd a broad smirk when he said that, broader still when some called him Godless. And Ned, he was all smiles, thinking he was going to find Ieuan ap y Gof. I ask you; there we are, setting off from our homes for an unknown land to fight the Welsh and Ned thinks he's going to meet up with his own Welshman that he hardly knows, just like that. But then, Ned always was an odd one.

He was my brother. That summer he'd have been near seventeen and that made me near eleven. Something like that. Ned was the one who knew about numbers. Some folk said he was daft but they didn't know nothing. They were the daft ones. Ned knew everything, more than anybody I've ever known, then or since. It's just that he didn't talk and if he tried it came out slurred, like he was drunk, and nobody could make out what he said. Except for me. I knew.

So we were at Boston Haven, the day after Lammas, boarding the boat that would take us up the Witham to Lincoln. We'd heard talk of Lincoln and what a fine town it was. From there we'd be marched to Chester, wherever that was. I'd no idea, then. And from there, well, God help us all. And what had we done to deserve it? We were fen men used to making land out of sea. King Edward reckoned we were just the men he needed and what Edward wanted, Edward got. He'd forgotten we were the men he'd tried to slaughter, ten years back. I was a bairn, it's true, when they'd drifted into our village for shelter but I heard talk. They'd been fighting old King Henry and Edward his son who they called 'the Leopard', but only behind his back. Even as a young man he had a violent temper. Everybody knows the tale about the young squire they say he quarrelled with. Ears cut off. Folk don't forget. He's done far worse, since. Far worse.

We had padded jerkins that the women made for us and we'd made weapons for ourselves, long staffs topped with little spearheads that wouldn't land a dab, let alone a man. It was the best we could do in the time. Our ditching tools looked more use. It was muddling, what with folk yelling and grabbing and shoving and the deck heaving and dipping under our feet and the sails spreading out and cracking in the wind. They said that the wind blowing around Boston was the devil struggling with the saint but I don't know about that. Still, the wharf was bobbing up and down and, above it, the great flat sky over the fen was bright blue. As far as you could see was blue sky and white sheep grazing on the green salt marsh, where there'd be sea in winter, and the birds were everywhere. The air was full of their din. The sea banks were sound, we'd made sure of that, but even so it was taking a risk. August, then September, then the storms. We looked after each other in the fen villages but there'd be only women and bairns and old men left with us digging men gone. The fighting men had left months back. Ralf was one of them. He was sixteen and a man, not a squibbling like me, he said, and I knew he meant it. We hadn't been friends that last year. He hadn't time for me anymore. Besides, I had our Ned to look out for. That's why I was going now, on the last boat – to look out for Ned, though I was but ten. There was no choosing, then; we were always together. And with me and Ned gone, there was only Mam and my three sisters. It didn't seem right. Dad was long gone, one fierce winter past. We didn't talk about him. As for me, I suppose I was gripped by it all. I didn't know any better. I didn't know what it meant. I was only ten and only knew the marshes and fens and now I was going out into the world, even if it was to war. So that made three of us glad to be going.

The winter had seemed endless the year he died and the seas rolled over the banks, threatening them all with destruction. They'd been repairing the bank when a freak wave caught the man unawares. They brought him back half drowned and frozen through. He caught a fever and shivered and shook for three days and nights. Then he died. The ground was so frozen they could hardly dig deep enough for a grave. Better wait for the thaw, someone said, but it seemed ungodly. Afterwards, his youngest son couldn't sleep. He lay listening, night after night, to the rumble and thud of the pounding tide and the wind – if it was the wind – wailing over the salt marsh. He thought of his father lying stiff in his shroud and wondered if a corpse felt the cold. And where was his soul? Brother John said he was a good father and a good husband and he deserved a place in heaven, but Mam always said he was bound for hellfire. Mam never lied. The boy could hardly breathe in the thick black night and he sat up, suffocating. Ned was there, next to him, tucking the blanket round him and stroking his hair. He lay down and fell asleep.

It was cramped on the boat. We sat huddled together, trying not to mind the pitching about. We might live with the sea at our door but we weren't used to being on it, except maybe for Harold Edmundson. The Northman had been blown in on one of the storms six winters ago, the only man found alive when the boat smashed on the sea wall. They thought he was a ghost at first, with his white hair and lashes and pale blue eyes and pale skin. He didn't speak our tongue and had never quite got the hang of it, even six years on. Never spoke a word about the shipwreck. There were eight of us from our village: as well as me and Ned and Peter Long and Harold Edmundson, there was John Thatcher and his son Dick, Walter Reed and Gilbert Allbone. I was wary of John Thatcher's sharp tongue, and sorry for Dick, a brawny young man who still had to bear the weight of his dad's tongue lashing, even though he was old enough to be wed, and had a mind to, but his mam was dead and there was no girl willing to wed the son because it meant looking after the father as well. That's what they said, anyway.

We were land men. We walked across water on stilts and went in flat-bottomed craft or we used the tracks that outsiders never knew about or could never find. That was how we'd kept safe, down the years. Not on a pitching boat. Ned, though, he was sat up, his black hair blown about in the wind and that beaky nose of his snuffing up the sea smells and his bright eyes watching the last of the loading and his ears soaking up the sounds. Then he was on his feet, pointing and smiling, and we heard the stamping of horse hooves and whinnying, and a voice we knew well. 'It's the young master,' the word went round, and we were glad because the squire's son was a good man, fair and just, even if he was still half grown. Well, that's what they said though he seemed manly to me; he must have been in his twenties, then. His boy was trying to lead the squire's horse up the boards and on to the boat, but the beast wasn't budging. It dug its front feet hard against the edge of the boards and reared back. Squire Phillip took hold of the bridle and pulled hard but it made no odds, though the horse threw up its head and rolled its eyes in pain. Squire Phillip was red in the face and bothered; then he must have caught sight of Ned's grinning face because he shouted up to him.

'You there! Down here now!' Ned scrambled down from his perch and edged across the crowded deck to where horse and master still battled. Beside me, I heard Peter groan and Walter's pipsqueak: 'Your Ned's in for it now.' Squire Phillip might be fair and just but he didn't stand any rubbish. I didn't answer. I just watched, wondering when I'd have to jump in and help.

'Boy! If what Brother John tells me is true, you can whisper me this poor beast on board.' Squire Phillip gave Ned the rein and he just stood there with it in his hands, not moving. We waited and watched. I don't think any of us took a breath. And still Ned did not move. But neither did Squire Phillip. And neither did the horse.

Now it was quiet, we realised what a bony beast it was, a bit of a nag, not a war horse at all, not a proper destrier. It put its head down and snorted and pawed the ground then just stood there, panting, its sides heaving. Ned waited. Slowly, he rested a hand on the horse's nose. Bony fingers on a bony beast, I thought; they were well matched, both on the gawky side and black maned. I settled back then. I could see what was bound to happen, but the rest of the men were still taut, watching.

They liked Ned, though he was odd. They didn't want him to come to harm. He was cooing to the horse now, in the tongue that was his own, a sort of gurgling from his throat. The horse lifted its head and its ears pricked. Its nostrils flared and its eyes slid sideways and fixed on Ned. He left the snaffle well alone. He took a step on to the boards and the horse followed. We didn't make a sound as the horse followed him up and on to the deck, bridle jingling and hooves clomping but as good as gold. Some of the sailors crossed themselves. We hutched up to make room for the beast. Nag or no, it had two strong back legs.

Squire Phillip came up on to the deck behind them. He wasn't a bit put out, like some of them would have been with their pride all mangled. He nodded at Ned. 'Keep him quiet,' was all he said. I wanted to laugh out loud, then, because I could see both their faces, horse and boy, and I swear they both nodded together, bright black eyes fixed on Squire Phillip, black manes blown back in the wind.

Squire Phillip had four men-at-arms with him, all well past their youth and all that the manor could muster. There were six hounds that looked as bony as the nag. The hounds flopped on the deck, panting, red tongues lolling. We hutched up again to make what room we could. Hounds of war? Our village curs were fiercer. A boy older than me and as scrawny as the dogs flopped down with them and wriggled himself against the soft belly of one of them. It nuzzled his ear then both boy and hound fell to scratching at fleas. I wanted to laugh again but then I was thinking about the old squire left behind while his son, the child of his old age, went to war. His first wife had died childless. He'd married again, a young girl barely ripe for wedding and bedding. When the son was born there was feasting in the village, better than any holy day. That's what they said. It happened long before I was born. The second bairn, a girl child, died before she took breath and the mother died with her. No more wives after that, and no more bairns. I wondered if the old squire had watched his one son walk away to war.

Then there wasn't time for wondering or for laughing because we'd slipped off from the wharf and were sailing up the river on the tide. There were onlookers on the wharf waving us off as they'd waved off boat after boat of men in the past months, all bound upriver for Lincoln. Ralf was one of them. He'd left early in spring and no one had had news of him. He was sixteen and well made. The girls loved him but he wanted Marie, a Gascon girl who had come by boat and stayed. She was a stranger to the village and the village girls didn't like it. When Ralf left, Marie had a hard life. He came back for her after the first war and took her away from the village. That's what they said. I wasn't there at the time. By the time I did come back, everything had changed. Everybody had changed. Or maybe it was just me.

Now there were three hundred of us fen men, they said, on our way to the Welsh war. Three hundred. I didn't know there were so many of us living so close together. I'd not enough fingers to count that many. I could see Peter's wench roaring into her apron and her belly swelled out like a wood pigeon stuffed full with food. 'Another deliverance?' I heard John Thatcher say. We all knew what he meant but only John would dare say so. He'd a tongue sharper than any of our ditching tools. Walter Reed's skinny wife was there, next to Winifred

Allbone: one was all bulging flesh, the other a tight shanks, just like their men, and both snuffling. Mam and my sisters were not there. They'd seen us off from the village. I looked back once. The girls were holding on to her skirt, the littlest one with her thumb stuffed in her mouth. Mam was staring after us, her face set like the skin on a two-day-old pudding. I didn't know whether she was more worried for herself and the lasses or for Ned. It wasn't for me. She'd only ever had a clout round the ear for me, if she could catch me. She said I ran her ragged, what with the fights I was in and the way I jawed at folk. And it was true, I did fight and I did have a mouth on me, just like her, but it was always because I was looking out for Ned. 'Look out for your brother.' It was almost the last thing she said to me but then, she'd been saying it all my life, ever since I could remember.

'Look out for him,' she'd warned, but how could he? He was so much younger, with stubby little legs, and his brother's legs were long, like a black-tailed godwit's, and just as agile at wading. Wait for me! His voice couldn't carry across that great, flat expanse of marshland. It was a gasp of air, breathless, piping like a curlew's call. His toe caught in a fallen stump and he stumbled and fell flat on his face, and he bawled, a pathetic bundle of snot and tears and mud and sodden clothing. Echoing in his ears was her voice, always with that rasp of command: 'Look out for him'. Above, clouds swirled black and blacker and the first fat drops of rain splashed on his face and plopped into the black pools of the marshes. A skulking snipe burst out from the sedge, rasping and sneezing its own warning. Look out! Look out! There was a shadow looming over him, tall and hunchbacked, like a heron, but it was his brother's hand reaching down, his brother's arms twining round him, sucking him up from the black marsh mud and holding him tight. It was the whole world in one face. He'd heard. He'd come back. Now they were both safe. And the sea could growl and prowl as much as it liked behind the wall. They were safe from the marsh devil, and she wouldn't shout and hit him.

We were quiet, watching the wharf, and our folk, fade out of sight. The sea wall lay behind us, and the thumping of sea waves. Now there was the growing heat of the sun and the hiss of the boat slicing through the river water and the slapping of little river waves against its sides. Fen gave way to marsh and marsh gave way to green fields and the long orchards of apple and pear trees, not planted too close together for fear of cutting off the breeze and doing harm to folks' health.

'They'll ripen before we're home,' someone said.

'If we come home at all.'

Did anyone speak the words? Or were we just thinking them…

A misty autumn morning before dawn; grass soaking wet and moisture dripping from the leaves of apple trees. He could hear it smacking from leaf to leaf and felt it splash cold on his forehead when he gazed up through the shadowy branches. The apples hung like small moons: round, plump, bound to be juicy, with that bite to them that the abbey apples always had. He imagined how they would taste in his mouth, then he hung back. This was how Eve was tempted.

'Come on,' Ralf whispered. 'We have to hurry. There'll be folk about soon.'

'We can't. It's stealing from God.'

'No it isn't. It's help from the Brothers. God doesn't eat apples.'

'Listen!'

They froze like rabbits, ears twitching. The first birds were stirring into song and a cow in the next meadow coughed. The grass rustled behind them. The shadow shifted, attenuated, became a lanky shape. Ralf yelped.

'It's all right. It's our Ned.'

'I said he shouldn't come.'

'He won't say nowt. You know he doesn't.'

'But I said.'

'Well, it's too late now.'

'Aye well, let's get on with it.'

They didn't take too many; just enough to carry back in one of Mam's blankets. When it was his turn to carry it, the apples were hard and knobbly against his back. He was glad Ned was there. It made it all right with God if Ned was there but he didn't say so to Ralf. Ralf wouldn't have understood.

We stared at our land sailing past us, glistening under the morning sun. Walter Reed coughed and worked on his throat, his Adam's apple bobbing. He was the oldest of us. When he was a young man he could turn more turf than any man in any of the villages round Swineshead. That's what they said. Now he did less and less but he knew his craft and there was many a man in our village taught by him. Even Peter Long said so. It didn't make me like him any more than he liked me, fusty old stick.

We sailed on into the afternoon, past abbey after abbey, lying on the banks of the broad Witham all looking peaceful and rich. Past Kirkstead, past the Priory of Stixwold, its iron works and its Prioress. Past Tupholme, the Isle of Sheep, and the canal that joined it to the Witham. The men who had dug the canal were joining us at Lincoln. They'd gone ahead of us that morning. That's what the sailors said. We sailed on past Bardney, on its little island, and I thought about the wronged saint shut out from the abbey. He came here like a beggar, they said, and he was told he could not go in. It was only later they found out that he was a saint and that they had made a terrible choice. They had shut the saint out of the abbey and out of their lives and their souls were lost. Who knows where God walks, or when, or how he looks? Sometimes thinking doesn't do you any good.

Do you come from Bardney?

Shut the door.

Keep it open.

It's not easy, choosing, and I feel pity for the monks. It's only afterwards that you can see the choice you should have made. It's only then that you know you've shut out the saint and the hope of salvation. At the time, you did what you did for the best. God help us all.

The lay brothers in the grain meadows waved at us and we waved back. They had hoisted up their gowns for coolness as much as for work and I could see a flash of flesh as they moved through the fields, scything the golden stalks. One of them had dropped his tunic from his shoulders and it hung from his waist. His skin was the nut brown of a man out in all weathers and he gleamed with sweat. Even his shaved head was shining. They were harvesting the first of the grain. Later, they would bind the stooks and stand them to dry, ready for winnowing. It was always a good crop here on the banks of the Witham; the summer had been hot and dry and the grain was fuller than it had ever been. Even on the boat I caught a snatch of its scent and my nose twitched.

To me, the journey was like one of our holidays when we would all go off to the fair, except this was better. Peter had drawn out some dice and gathered a crowd about him. I listened to them laughing and shouting and laying their bets and the rattle of dice on the wooden deck of the boat. If I'd had pennies to bet, I'd have laid them on Peter. He knew every move there was. Even when he was caught – and he always was – he found a way out. I knew he'd fleece Gilbert Allbone who was big and broad and fleshy, not bone at all. He was a good ditcher, but he'd not much of a brain and was as trusting as a child. They said he was called Allbone because one dry summer, he'd found a body in one of the dried-up marsh pools: it was a man, his flesh blackened by the marsh mud, looking new dead but he had no bones. Plenty of hair and with fingernails and all, but no bones. He was nothing but a bag of wrinkled skin. Some said it was finding the boneless body that fuddled Gilbert Allbone's brain but I don't think so. We turned up stranger things than men's bodies when we were ditching. Besides, his mother was odd. A bit of the witch in her, Mam used to say. Big Gilbert was called 'Allbone' after that as a joke. He didn't seem to mind. I watched for a while until I saw pennies pass from Gil to Peter then I edged up to Ned and the nag.

'Keeping him quiet, then?'

He grinned at me and the horse blew down his shirt and nuzzled into his hand.

'Where's the snaffle?'

He pointed to a heap on the deck. It said something for Squire Phillip, that he used a snaffle and not a curb. One more reason to be glad he was with us.

We watched the land sliding by, and the brown water sloshing against the keel of the boat and rippling out behind us. The land was changing again and little rounded hills reared up in front of us now. Like the breasts of a young girl, Peter Long said, but then, that's what he would say. He had women on the brain. If he wasn't laying a bet, he was laying a woman, they said in the village. I'd heard them. They laughed like it was a joke but they kept their daughters well away from him. The girl on the wharf wasn't from our village.

I can't remember what I was thinking. I was not quite eleven and it was a long time ago. Maybe I was thinking about Aelfwyn, my older sister's friend. She was little and fair and smelled sweet as honey and I'd started thinking about her a lot, that spring. Maybe I was thinking about her when Peter said that about the hills. I wonder, now, what Ned was thinking. Maybe nothing.

We sailed on, late into the afternoon. We passed a boat loaded with stone from one of the quarries. Some abbey would be waiting for it. They kept building and building, war or no war. There was even new building at our church. Ned and me, we'd crept in and seen it. All the fine carving, like it was real.

Quietly, shifting like shadows on a wall in summer sunshine, they'd edged towards the opening. One was elongated, like a skeleton; the other shorter, closer knit.

'Where?'

The whisper echoed around the empty space and up to the vaulted ceiling. The skeleton beckoned and the squat shape followed. The pillars in the nave were long, slender stems and their tops, or capitals, were cushioned on carved heads. The squat shape stared: he recognised the faces. There was Harold Baker with his puffy cheeks; Eric Smith, eyebrows raised, all surprised, just like he did when he didn't want to answer; Godwin Salter looking innocent when everyone knew he wasn't. There were others. It was a miracle. He laughed and his laughter echoed in God's space and, behind it, echoed the other's laughter, a bit rusty, like a voice that wasn't often used.

We were drowsy with sun and the dip and pull of the boat. Even the dice players had stopped. I watched the bank until it all blurred, and I slept – curled up on the deck like a brown rat, John Thatcher said later. Lucky, he added, the hounds hadn't sniffed me out and gobbled me up. I looked at the hounds and their bony flanks and wondered when they had last been hunting and what they had fed on. Poor devils, our village dogs had a better life. Poor old squire, with little enough to live on and his son gone to war, duty bound to

Edward. And John Thatcher was a halfwit if he thought to frighten me.

It was almost dark. We were at the wharf-side and there were torches and a jumble of voices and folk on the move. It stank of rot and dung and things gone bad. There was a muddle of buildings. High above us, higher than anything I'd seen, was a great dark mass, heavy against the darkening sky and, even darker, on top of it was the outline of castle walls and bulky keep. It crowded us, used as we were to flat land and space. Even the dark seemed different. The others felt it too. I heard John Thatcher mutter, spade sharp, to his son: 'Best wake up what wits you've got, lad, in a place like this.'

We docked and suddenly it was like cold wind blowing in winter. Like I said, we were men used to making land from the sea and doing it our way. We weren't used to taking orders. Now there was a sergeant-at-arms bellowing like a bull – a heifer, John muttered – and hurrying us off the boat, drilling us into rows.

'Line up. Twos. Straighten up. Heads up. Chins up.'

His chest heaved in a long sigh.

'Try to look smart, you scum. King Edward wants an army, not a bunch of wankers, you Fenland pillocks.'

We shuffled into a row, in twos. I had pins and needles from being curled up so long and I saw others stumble. The sergeant-at-arms stalked us, smirking. He could have saved himself the breath; we were Fenlanders and used to insults. We'd lived with them for years. Water off a shelduck's back. Then he stopped at Ned.

'God save us, a fen fucking idiot.'

Ned grinned, his long body slopping into its usual hunched

heron shape. I could feel myself bristling, just waiting for it, waiting to punch the pisspot right in his scabby face. Look out for our Ned? I'd been doing that all my life. I was gritting my teeth, getting my fists ready when Dick Thatcher nudged me in the ribs.

'Say nowt, young Will. Best left.'

Beyond him, John Thatcher muttered, 'What a stench – fart breath.'

Walter Reed sucked in his breath; he'd seen me take off before now and he didn't like it, the sour mouth. In front of me, the Northman tripped over some coiled rope and staggered against big Gil. The sergeant-at-arms skipped up to them.

'Clumsy pillocks. Stand up. Straight!'

He moved on. Harold Edmundson turned and winked. I stretched my fingers and felt them crack. Next to me, Ned was still grinning his idiot's grin and I wanted to yell at him. Can't you see what they think? Can't you try to look normal? Why are you making it so hard for us? But I didn't. I never did.

And then we were marching, one two, one two, from the wharf to a stretch of flat ground near the riverbank. 'Camp here for the night. Up tomorrow at dawn. Wait here for orders.' It's all a blur, now, the camp, the bad food, the hard ground under canvas.

That was the first night away from our village and I suppose I should remember it better but I can't. Not now. Since then there have been too many hard beds and often no food and only the night sky and the star blanket for cover. I couldn't think straight, then, what with the journey and being so worn out and the strangeness of it all. What I do remember is that dark mass looming above us, and Dick Thatcher saying in that quiet way of his: give us a song, Ned. Ned breathing into the swan pipe and the notes breathing back at us and it sounded like the marsh birds and the wind and the sea surge. I could almost see the waves shining in the dark with the stars and I was thinking that these were the same stars we had in the fens. Then Peter Long was grinning and pulling out a wad of stuff. 'Want some?' he asked. And we could smell dried eels, like home. And, since home seemed a far off land, we gulped down what he had.

It wasn't the first time I'd heard the dawn song. I was awake long before that and so was Ned. I could hear him breathing, like he was wide awake. Sometimes I wondered if he ever slept.

I whispered. 'Ned?'

I knew he could hear me. I knew he was awake. When I crawled out of my blanket, he was there. We walked out together. We were in an old camp, Roman, they said. Lincoln was a Roman camp. I don't know. This was a square of land with bothies and bits of wall, well built at one time. One stretch was almost fifteen feet high, I guessed, with a clay mound banking it. Stone robbers would have a hard time taking pieces from it. But then I forgot all that and gaped open-mouthed, like a seagull, because there was Lincoln high on a steep crag. It was the black mass of last night. We could see the line of the castle clear now and, a throw away, the new church that they were building after fire ruined the old one. It was huge. I thought our abbey church was big enough but this was different. It looked like a ship sailing out over the hilltop, proud and free. It wasn't even half-built then, but you could see straight away what it was going to look like when all the scaffolding was down and the tower was finished. I've seen it since and it's a wonderful church in the making, but I feel different now I know it was bonded with the blood of men who died in the making of it, working men like us. But that morning, well, Ned and me thought it was wonderful, like something out of an old tale, and we were part of it. I felt like I was going to be a hero.

By early morning, we were marching north. It was a steep climb up that great hill. We marched past houses built of heavy stone blocks, solid-looking houses, in the old style. I wouldn't have taken note but Walter Reed piped up, 'That's where the Jews live.'

'Not for much longer, if the Leopard has his way,' John Thatcher's voice was grim.

'Time they were kicked out. Can't trust 'em – never could,' said one of the Axholme men. 'Remember what happened? Murderers. Murder us all in our beds, they would.'

'That was twenty years ago, man, and they were innocent. Everyone knows that.' John Thatcher sounded edgier than ever then he added, oddly for him, 'Poor devils'.

I remembered John Thatcher's words not many years after that, when Edward drove the Jews out of Lincoln and all England. But I didn't know what he meant then and there was too much to take in.

We were on the old straight road marching north out of the town. I remember there was a great arch ahead of us, curving over the road; part of an old wall. And there was a second, smaller arch for ordinary folk to walk through. We went through the great arch, marching two by two, like real men of war. I was swell-chested, what with all the townsfolk looking on. By now, we were three hundred and more and we had three pisspots ordering us about, all on horseback, and all of them devils-in-waiting. We couldn't tell one from the other. They were all squat and broad with greasy hair and they talked bad English and worse Norman, so Peter Long said. They were angry with us, he said, because we were scum, riding on the tail of the fighting men. The hard work had been done over the spring and summer.

'Just mopping up, now, that's what they say,' Peter told us. He was the only one on friendly terms.

'We'll not be shedding overmuch blood, then,' said John Thatcher.

Squire Phillip was nowhere to be seen and that was a blow. Instead, we were led by a man with the face of a kestrel, and a watchfulness to match.

'That's Master William of March,' Peter Long said, but he didn't tell us any more, which was odd for him, and I saw he kept his head down.

'He's the master *fossatore*,' Dick Thatcher told me, and the Latin word sounded odd in his mouth, though I'd heard it before. It was the word the big men used when they needed the craft of us little men: the ones who knew how to dig ditches, keep the sea out, and make the land grow. *Fossatore*. Ditch digger. It was all the same to us. I'd heard tell of Master William, another big man, and a builder; he was the one rounding us up. He'd already been as far as Chester, so they said.

'Then back he came to find more damned souls for his army of ditch diggers,' John Thatcher said to anyone who was listening, and spat.

We should have been mutinous but it was a sunny morning and the birds were singing and there was adventure in the air, in spite of the stench of rot and dung. I was young. My belly was full because of Peter's eels and the gruel they'd fed us for breakfast and I was ready to go.

We marched all morning under the high crag, heading north on the old road then west along a good road towards the great river, the one they called the Trent. We were headed for a town called Torksey, where the Trent met the Fossdyke and where there was a ferry that had been running many years and did a good trade in tolls. We learnt that much from some of the others who'd arrived before us. They came from Axholme Fenland, further north still, and they knew the Trent. When we stood on the edge of the river and saw how broad it was, and how it tumbled between its banks, we understood and were grateful for a safe crossing place even though there was some fun made about what we were worth. After all, like Peter said, this was our rival. If trade didn't come through Boston, it came up the Trent and the Fossdyke.

'Eight sheep a penny,' someone snorted. 'How much is that for three hundred?'

And then we were truly into strange lands.

Two

The firmament does not change. It does not know time. It is perfect and eternal. Inside the indivisible circle are the seven spheres, and that makes eight. At the centre, safe kept, is the ninth sphere, and that is earth. Here the four elements – earth, water, fire, air – forever mingle and separate. Here, everything is subject to time and change. Here, all is inconstant, unstable. Listen. At the centre of all things, listen. Everything has its note. Everything has its sound. And when all is in proportion, then there is harmony, and we are happiest.

I had drowned, and my body was at the bottom of the green sea. Far above, waves were hissing and hussing but down here it was very still. I was at rest. Harold Edmundson was a hand's breadth away, bleached face turned towards me. So this is what it is like, Northman, I was thinking. I wondered if he truly thanked us for saving his body from the sea. His mouth was open and his breathing was warm on my face. That was when I knew we were not dead after all, but sleeping. It was the great forest that sighed about us, not waves, and we were far from the sea and far from our homes.

That night we had made camp inside the boundary wall of Rufford, bedding down wherever there was room between the stinking tannery and the woolhouse. Master William ate at the Abbot's table and slept in a clean bed.

'All right for some,' John Thatcher muttered.

'We are not forgotten. We have a good supper and bread to take with us, friend,' Harold Edmundson chided gently.

'And honey.' Gil Allbone sighed and I sighed with him, thinking of the sweet honey cakes our monks made; not much hope of tasting those here. We were glad to be safe on abbey land that belonged to the white monks, like at home; even the layout of the buildings was the same. It always was, Brother John had said, and it was true; Ned and me, we could have found our way about blindfold, and none the wiser but God.

'Same, but not the same,' I warned Ned, 'so don't go wandering.'

Around us, the forest whispered and muttered. There was a hunter's moon that night; shadows lurked and small things squealed and there were giants with horns stretching high into the sky. Gil Allbone's eyes rolled in his head. I saw Walter Reed cross himself.

'Only trees, lads,' Dick Thatcher said. 'They're stag oaks – the top branches look like horns; that's all it is. Nothing to worry about.'

But we did. We were used to tidy orchards and big skies and flat land. Here, the boles of the trees showed strange shapes, like faces with staring eyes, shouting out stems and leaves from their mouths, like the one Ned had shown me in our church. Lichen bunched and swelled from every branch like shaggy hair. Not one of us was willing to slip away into the forest and flee home, although I'd heard whispers of such a thing. I was thinking Master William must have had this in his mind when he ordered that we camp here. We huddled round the camp fires and slept close to each other.

It was not long till daybreak. I heard the bell clanging for Vigils; soon it would clang again for Lauds. When it did, we would be kicked out of our sleep and the long day's march would begin again. The darkness was shifting already. A shape loomed to my left. It was Ned the sleepless, the wanderer. I rolled over and sat up.

'Where are you going?' I mouthed the words, not daring to speak aloud.

He grinned, his teeth showing white and his eyes gleaming in the dark. I didn't want to move. I wanted to stay safe in my nest of a bed but Ned shifted away out of my sight so I had to follow, trying not to stumble over the sleepers and snorers. I crept past the pisspot set to watch us, but he was asleep as well, his snout twitching and grunting and drool oozing from the corner of his mouth. I followed Ned out of the safe walls, keeping close, too used to his ways to be amazed that it was easy for him. I wondered what they'd do to us if we were found out, and if there was any tale we could tell to keep us safe. I wasn't thinking about the still and silent wood. I kept all thoughts of that out of my mind. Tall grass smeared wet streaks on my bare legs and branches showered dew. Everything smelt of damp moss and bracken.

We stopped near a spinney of birch trees, their trunks ghosting the gloom. The dark forest with its horned giants was outlined now against a sky the hue of Master William's war sword. I shivered with cold and fear and it was only because it was Ned that I stayed. He was waiting, listening. Far off, the abbey bell called for Lauds. The sky grew paler and the first birds stirred. First the turtle doves, cooing high up in the tree tops; then the ground birds' harsh cry; then the twittering of hedge birds swelled round the woodland until the sound burst inside my head so that I forgot my fear and the cold and wet. I forgot the pisspots and William the Kestrel and the strange faces in the boles of the trees. I forgot the long march to war. There was only Ned and me in the cool green wood listening to the daybreak. I looked at him, but in the dimness I could hardly set him apart from the trees. It was like that morning we had crept into the church of the white monks.

They hid behind the cloister door; then sneaked inside. The work was finished; a forest of pillars had rooted itself in the nave. It was not like the church in the village; there were no windows like coloured jewels, or Judgement Day terror leaping from the walls, or Harold Baker and Eric Smith and Godwin Salter for ever and ever straining to hold up the roof. Here were austere white walls and undecorated pillars in perfect proportion; that was the way of the white monks.

He couldn't see the brothers from his hiding place but he heard the soft rustle as they took their places for Lauds. Their voices travelled up into the high vaulting of the transept and alleluia filled the plain space, the echoes of it resonated and reverberated and floated around him in a thousand voices, a thousand times richer than the richest gold leaf. He couldn't think. He didn't care if they were caught and punished. His soul was caught in the echoing ecstasy and tossed about in the body of the church.

At last Ned and me crept back into the camp. No one knew we were gone. We marched all day along the old paths and I saw now that this was an ordered world, though not like the fens. The strips were bright with grain, ready to harvest. Barley heads shone white in the sun and they dipped and swayed like the sea on the shore on a calm day. In some of the strips, reapers were already at work, and the sun glinted on their upraised scythes. The fields were bounded by ditches and beyond were orchards of gnarled crab apples set with fruit and groves of wych elm, neatly coppiced. We marched down a hollow way hedged with hazel and snatched at the green nuts to see if they made good eating, chewing their milky softness as long as we could. Charcoal-makers were hard at work but they laid off what they were doing to stare at us as we went by, not quite so lively as we had been when we strutted out of Lincoln. Our feet were blistered and our bodies ached and the sun was too hot in a sky that had no clouds. Heat rose up from the ground and our feet and faces felt as if they were on fire. Ahead of us, the land stretched into blue distance but with no salt sea to meet the sky. I'd never seen so far without the sea in sight.

We passed a lad herding pigs. He was about my age and his mouth gaped wide at the sight of three hundred marching men and pack horses and the sergeants on their nags following behind a Norman lord astride a real warhorse with cold, jangling harness. He gaped even wider, like a cod fish, when he saw me and I nearly made a rude sign at him. I was thinking how it was that some folks kept to their ways, like the white monks, and, for others, life shifted like elf lights on the marsh. I wondered what it would be like for that lad to change places with me.

It seemed that everything got higher the further we marched. First it was Lincoln, then the tall trees like giants, and now there were great crags and high peaks that loomed over us and would crush us if they fell. We kept on, that day, marching straight towards them, and they grew taller and taller and darker and darker until they blotted out the sky and the setting sun and we were in their shadow. The men started to mutter, loud enough this time for the pisspots to hear.

'It's better looking out across the fens and the sea wall,' Walter Reed grumbled. 'I don't like this looking up at everything. It gives me a crick in my neck and a pain in my side.'

'You're nowt but a crick in the neck and a pain in the side,' John Thatcher cut back, 'so mebbe you'll spare a thought for the rest of us now.'

Everyone laughed because it was true; Cerdic Little, one of the Tupholme men, nicknamed him 'Water Rod', because he was always stopping to piss, grunting away though there was nothing but a trickle came out of him. Stephen Fowler – the one who'd called the Lincoln Jews murderers – called him 'Walter Greed', because he tried to snaffle more than his share at every meal. Walter Reed sucked in his mouth, like he'd been eating sour apples, and looked straight ahead and said nothing. I started to laugh as well but then I thought about his skinny wife snuffling on the wharf and the way his Adam's apple bobbed up and down as he watched the fens slip further and further away. It was bobbing now, like a sour apple stuck there. I didn't laugh. It's not easy, choosing, but it's better than having no choice. I felt pity for him. He was the oldest of us.

'Play us a tune, Ned,' Dick Thatcher said, 'something to keep us in good spirits. Something we can sing to.'

'I can't sing. I haven't a note in me.' Stephen Fowler hawked and tried to spit. 'My mouth's as dry as an old maid's hole.'

'Needs working on, then,' said Dick. He wasn't flustered by anything, Dick Thatcher wasn't, and I liked him for it. He made you feel safe. Ned wasn't flustered either, but with Ned you were never sure what he would do next. Nor was he fussed, like the rest of us, by the heat or the long march or the strange shape of the land. Now he did what Dick asked and played us along the way, and we marched along croaking out the songs as if they'd keep us safe from the great crags, with their shadows like devils leaning over us.

And in the end we didn't have to walk over the top of the world. Master William called us together and told us, in his posh Norman voice, that we'd skirt the high land. We were such a poor lot of fenland dolts, too used to easy fenland ways; we'd never make it through the sheer rock passes. Our King had journeyed across the high roads many times, but he was a soldier king, manly, with a man's pride. We were weak, snivelling scum so we'd take the long way round and walk faster and longer. At least, that's not quite what he said but it's what he meant. One of the pisspots was giving a free translation, Peter Long told us. He wasn't quite so friendly with them now.

And that's what we did: we rose earlier and rested later and walked longer and faster, and were glad to be skirting the edge of the high land until it lay behind us. I'd never seen any land so tall. I didn't know, then, that it would seem as nothing before many months passed.

That last night, we camped in the bailey of Nantwich castle. We'd be in Chester early the next afternoon, travelling easily along one of the roads the salt traders used. And after that – well – nobody liked to think. We were all worried and stirred up and there was a lot of uneasy laughing and joking. I don't know who started the singing but suddenly we were belting out 'Merry it is while summer lasts', though it wasn't a merry song but sad.

'Not as if we've got much to be merry about, God knows,' John Thatcher said, but he growled along with us all the same. Someone started griping about the Feast of Assumption and how we'd miss it, being only a week away. After that, there was a lot more joking about the dancing at the feast and the way the women were, even the old ones with withered bodies. Peter Long played at being an old hag, hitching his skirts up above his arse and warbling, 'Embrace me with the rushes green' and throwing himself at Walter Reed who squealed like a silly girl and fell backwards. Peter Long was yelling, 'the sin of touching – the sin of touching', and I was sure his hands were all over Walter Reed because of his squeaking and squealing and cursing. We were all guffawing, even the pisspots, and I was thinking how good it was to be one of the men. I wondered where Ralf was and what he was doing. Then somebody said, 'Have you heard this one?' So we sat round listening to riddles that had been told time after time; everybody knew the answers but it was the telling that mattered. We were the loudest group, and it wasn't long before others drifted away from their own fires to join us. Everybody likes to laugh.

Peter Long knew all the riddles. He stood up to tell the one about the dough.

'I have heard of – something or other.' And he smirked and closed one eye with such a lewd look on his face that we choked and howled. 'Swelling and rising, pushing up its covering.' He had one hand up under his skirts, his fist making the cloth rise. He waited for the groans and more howls to die away. 'And on that boneless thing a cocky-minded young woman took a grip with her hands and with her apron covered the swelling thing.' And his other hand came down to clutch the risen cloth and his fist under it.

Every man clapped and stamped and their eyes were bright, and their silly grins made me think how they missed their women. Even Walter Reed was smiling but his eyes were sad and I was thinking again about the snuffling, bony woman who was his wife.

Then Thomas Wytheberd of Bardney stood up. He told the tale of one of the old heroes. He told it well. I looked at the faces of the men round the fire in the twilight. I had listened to tale tellers many times before and wondered at the way they gripped hold of their listeners. I knew what it was to spin tales myself and make folk believe them. But here were men who were frightened of what the day would bring, taking heart from the old tales, and sergeants who had cursed us for fools listening now like children. We were no longer foes and I thought it was sharing the tales and laughter that had made it so.

Afterwards, someone turned to Ned. 'Play for us, Ned.' Other voices took it up, for it was well known now that the odd, lanky youth with the thatch of dark hair played like an angel. He grinned and brought out the swan pipe and played on it the bird sounds of the forest we had walked through, so that we laughed with wonder and begged for more. So he played the sound the wind made whistling through the great crags, even on a still summer's day, and it seemed their shadow fell on us again. Then he played only for us, and we heard the push and pull of the sea on the shore and the sad call of a sea bird mourning his mate so that Walter Reed's eyes grew wet and Gil Allbone sighed and even John Thatcher shut his mouth and shut his eyes, like he was in pain.

He stood there on the fen track, a hunched heron clutching the swan pipe to him and watching, watching until the short, round-shouldered man and the slight, graceful youth were long out of sight, disappeared into the raw February morning. He stayed there, still and silent, and on his face such misery that the boy didn't know how to comfort him. At last he said, 'You have the swan pipe, Ned.'

It was as if he hadn't spoken. Ned's face was closed against him; his eyes were dark gaps of nothingness, like those of a dead creature.

The boy thought a moment then started again. 'Remember what he said, Ned? It has magic. Remember the day he gave you the wing? "Birds are fallen angels," he said. Remember how he helped you make it into a pipe, Ned?'

He talked on, weaving the words into the story of how the two of them, the thin-faced, black-haired boy and the music master with hair red as flames, bent over the task for hours and hours, working in harmony and working harmony into the pipe. The two of them cleaned the hollow bone, inside and out, until it gleamed like moonshine; then the careful measuring and drilling of seven magic holes that the notes would breathe through, four low and three high; then the mouthpiece, bevelled securely to the distal end of the gleaming bone. At last, it was done.

'Then Ieuan ap y Gof, who called himself the servant of music, raised the swan pipe to his lips and breathed life into the dead bone until it sang like the angel it had once been.'

There was silence still, but its quality was different and there was a little less misery in the dark face next to him.

'Remember, Ned, he taught you to do the same. He said, whenever you played the pipe, it would be like a thread joining you both, body and soul.'

Ned's gaze didn't waver from the point where the two specks had vanished into the air, but he held the pipe lightly now, his fingers caressing the smooth bone. Then he raised it as he had been taught and a thread of wavering notes spilled out into the cold air.

We didn't make Chester so easily after all. We set off with the dawn and the rising sun behind our backs. We passed the salt houses Nantwich was known for and crossed the river that they called the Weaver because of the way it moved across the land. Late that morning, one of the nags cast a shoe. That didn't go down very well with the pisspot that had to walk with the rest of us and, to tell the truth, I felt sorry for him. He was fond of the mare and didn't want to cause her pain. Ned walked with him, stroking her side and murmuring his slurred sounds. The pisspot looked at him strangely at first then shook his head and seemed not to mind. When he spoke to me, I was startled. I didn't think any of them knew I was alive.

'They say he is your brother.' His speech sounded like Marie, Ralf's girl, so I guessed he was from Gascony. It was odd, throaty, not like the Norman tongue. I had to listen carefully.

'Yes.'

'Lost his wits, has he?'

I could feel the anger rising, as always, but then I saw he was just asking.

'No,' I added, though I knew he wouldn't believe me. 'He's clever, is Ned. He just doesn't talk much.'

'Ah,' was all he said and he was quiet a while. He tramped along in time with his nag. I could see sweat beading his forehead and the way the gritty dust clung to his beard. The wind was whipping up little eddies of dust around us and the heat was beating back from the uneven road that seemed to go on and on until I thought we would never get to Chester.

'He plays well. How did he learn?'

'From the white monks.'

I didn't think it wise to say that Ned had learnt from a Welshman, sworn enemy of the King and loyal to the death to Llewelyn ap Gruffudd. I added, because it was true, 'He's always whittled pipes. When I was little, he made them for me, from elder stems, but I could never get them to sing. Ned could. He has the knack.'

'The knack?' He puzzled over the word.

I thought a moment. 'The skill.'

'Ah.' He was quiet again then he gazed down at me, and his look was kind. 'You're a long way from home, boy. No complaining. I've noticed. You've done well.'

I didn't know what to say. I couldn't call him a pisspot any more, now he was like a man. I think I blushed.

'Your name, boy?'

'Will.'

He laughed. 'That is my name, also. Guillaume, like the Conqueror.'

'Not William,' I told him. 'My name is Wilfred. It's an English name, and my brother is Edmund, named after the saint.' I couldn't keep the pride from my voice and he laughed again.

'So, English Will. I have a boy at home about your age. A good boy, like you.'

We walked on, not speaking, both of us thinking our own thoughts. His, I guessed, were back at his home in Gascony and the boy about my age who was his son and, no doubt, the woman who was his wife. I wondered how long it would be before he got back to them. If he got back at all. And I thought how it was the same for him as for us. Same, but not the same.

The sun was high in the sky before we heard the far-off clanging of the smithy. Heat was shimmering above the roof and black smoke was lying on the air. There was the sound of hammering on the anvil.

'The forge is the heart of the smithy and the anvil is its soul.'

The music master's red hair flamed like the furnace itself. He had to raise his voice above the clamour.

'The blacksmith is the only worker who uses all four elements: iron and coal from the earth; fire to heat the iron and shape it to his will; air to make the fire burn hotter; water to harden the metal.'

He laughed in that way he had, as if he knew the boy was half afraid of him. Ned wasn't. Ned was earth, water, fire, air, yielding to the music master's will. The boy retreated from the heat and the noise and the spits of flame, back to the open door and watched the black-haired youth and the red-headed man from there, seeing the sparks that flew about them. It felt as if the hammers were resonating through the length of his own body and bursting his head open. In time with the strokes, he heard the man's voice.

'Listen to the sounds of the different hammers. This is what Pythagoras heard. Can you hear it? Different notes according to their weight. It's all in the numbers, of course.' He laughed again, and was echoed by the boy standing next to him.

The smithy was ramshackle, like the hovel that leant against it. The blacksmith was a woman. She was making a nail, holding the iron in pincers on the anvil and pounding out the four sides from the two sides. Behind her, a boy was half-heartedly squeezing bellows into the open mouth of the furnace. She straightened up and placed the nail back in the fire. I could see she was well set, despite the black that covered her face and arms and grimed her hands. Her hair was carefully bound up out of harm's way and the blacksmith's apron covered a rusty hemp gown that might once have been green. She didn't look awkward before us men. She didn't smile, either. She rubbed her hands on the apron. I wondered if she was rubbing grime off her hands or on to them.

'You'll be wanting to speak with my father,' she said. 'I'll get him for you.' She called something into the dark corner of the building and a man shuffled forward out of the shadows. His face was pale, like the parchment the monks write on, and his left hand was holding his right, and that was wrapped in coarse cloth and spotted with blood. He held it up to Master William.

'It's bad, sir,' he whined. 'I can't work today, sir.' His voice was loutish and the words slurred on his tongue.

Master William's sharp eyes swivelled from father to daughter and I saw now that she was younger than I had first thought, though her face was worn and tired.

'It seems there's no need for you to work any day, smith,' he said, and there was sharpness in his voice as well. I could smell the stale stench of ale about the man and I was thinking it was not the hand that kept him from work.

'This sergeant's horse has cast a shoe. We must reach Chester today.'

'Do you have the shoe with you, sir? It would be quicker if you had, sir.'

'We kept it.'

'Then you'll not have a long wait, sir, I'll make sure of that, sir.' He spoke over his shoulder to his daughter without turning his head. 'Winifred, see to it.'

The woman silently set about the task, urging the boy to work the bellows. Ned stayed, watching and listening, but I sat outside where there was air to breathe and shade to sit in. I was thinking again how nothing was the same, for any of us, and I wondered if life would shift for her, like the elf lights. I hoped it would. Maybe he would drink himself into his grave and then she would not be keeping the wretch in idleness and strong ale. Ned came round the back of the smithy and I wondered where he'd been. He squatted next to me and I saw he had stems of elder in his hands and a thin wire he must have cadged from the smith. He prodded at the soft pith inside the elder stem until it was clean. It was soothing, sitting there with him by me, out of the heat of the sun, and I let myself drift and dream.

Autumn on the marsh; rain clouds low on the horizon and crows tumbling in a windy sky. Far off, the roar of the sea pounding against the sea wall. They sat in the shelter of a bank of elder trees. They'd been picking the berry heads for Mam and the baskets were full of their bright blackness. They stank of elder, like tomcat piss, he thought. Ned had taken a handful of thick stems and was whittling away, whittling away until the bark was clean off. He cut a slit halfway through the stem, a little way in from one end, and another, in a V shape, so there was an opening like the leper squint in the church wall.

The boy watched him, marvelling as he always did at the sureness of the strokes. He knew what came next; Ned always carried bits of wood that would do for a plug – a twig of elm or beech or a piece of dowel begged from Edric Carpenter – and in it would go, fitting tight inside the squint end of the stem. Then Ned would cover the open end and blow. Sometimes, it sounded clear and bright but other times it made a sound like a fart and the boy would giggle and make his own farting noises. Ned would push the plug in and out and check the breathing channel then try again.

That windy afternoon, Ned made two pipes and gave one to him and they blew them together. His made a gasping sound, a hiss of breath behind the teeth, but Ned's was bright and clear and the boy knew that, even if they swopped pipes, he would never make his sing or startle the hedge birds with its sound.

'Will, come on, time to go.' Dick Thatcher was shaking me awake. Everyone was on the move, back on the road in the straggling line we made. Master William was at the front and as restless and fidgety as his horse. The sergeant who'd met us at Lincoln wharf was skipping about again. I knew his name now. Bogo. I could hear him bellowing, just like he did then, though he'd been in the first row to listen to the tale telling.

'Line up. Straighten up. Heads up. Chins up. What's the matter with you, you scumbags? You've had a nice long rest, you wankers. Time to pick your feet up.'

It was mid afternoon. Clouds were heaping up in the west and the sun kept dipping behind them. I shivered suddenly. When I tried to get up, my body was stiff and awkward. Dick Thatcher helped me up. 'Not far now, Will.' He sounded worried and I realised it was for me, the youngest. 'We'll get there before curfew, you'll see.'

I nodded. 'Where's Ned?'

'Giving gifts,' Dick said and his voice was dry. I looked round. Ned was edging crabwise up to the door of the smithy, nodding his head and grinning, and I groaned.

‘I’ll have to get him before the pisspots see.’

But it was too late. The one called Guillaume was there, with the new-shod nag, and I saw his hand go out and tap Ned on his arm. Ned turned, and I saw his own hand go out and in it was one of the pipes he’d been whittling away at. The sergeant looked puzzled when Ned gurgled something at him. I’d slipped through the ranks of men and up to them before Dick could stop me. Ned gurgled again.

‘It’s for you,’ I told the Gascon, ‘to take home to your son.’ He looked at the elder pipe in Ned’s hand. Ned put the pipe to his mouth and blew into it. The note caught on the air and mixed with the swallows’ chittering. Then the Frenchman was smiling and nodding, for all the world as if he had caught the trick from Ned, and he tucked the pipe inside his tunic as if it was a gold piece.

I looked at the second pipe and back at Ned. ‘He wants to give it to the smith woman.’

‘So he shall.’ The man called Guillaume spoke in his own tongue to the sergeant nearest to him, another Gascon, and the man shrugged and went back into the smithy. The woman came out. She looked hot and tired and eased her shoulders as if she ached, which I reckon she did, and her eyes were wary as she looked at the two sergeants.

‘A gift, madame, from the boy here,’ Guillaume said but I don’t think she understood his speech because she just stared at him, her face empty.

So I piped up, ‘My brother Ned’s made you this, miss.’ I stopped when that empty stare met mine. Behind me, the men watched and some were sniggering and any moment Master William would want to know what was going on. But there was Ned standing next to me, hunch shouldered, grinning like a silly child and holding out the crude pipe of elder. I couldn't let him down, not for all the King's men. I had no choice. I swallowed. 'He says it's for you because you are skilful and…' I stopped and gulped and ended in a rush, '…your eyes are as lovely as the summer day.'

And then I saw a miracle happen in front of my eyes. She stretched out her grimy hand with its blackened, torn nails, took the pipe and held it up in front of her. I saw her whole face soften and her eyes, that had been lifeless, were smiling and now I saw they were bright blue, and it was just as Ned said; they were lovely, like the summer day. Like periwinkles half hidden in the shade. Like the coloured windows in our church when the sun shone through them.

'Twos. Straighten up. Forward!'

She stood watching us until we were out of sight. I know. I kept turning back to look.

Three

Lift your face to the summer wind. Let it breathe over you. It is God's breath, maker of the first music. Listen to it thrum in the rigging of the boats. It is the invisible harpist. Watch how the reeds bend to the wind's song. The wind breathes itself into them, so that they, too, sing in harmony. Life is held together by breath. When breath stops, so does life.

The sun was low in the sky as we came to Chester. It lay behind a bank of cloud, setting the whole sky ablaze.

'Longshanks' set fire to all of Wales,' someone joked.

'Or soaked it in blood,' John Thatcher said.

The earth there is red, and the stone; and the walls of Chester were red like the sky. We fell silent.

'It's an omen,' Walter Reed said, and nobody jeered.

The road was busy with traders hurrying to beat the curfew. Just before we came to the place where the roads meet, by Gallow's Hill, a great cloud of dust came rolling towards us, followed by the noise and clatter of herded cattle. The drovers kept up a deafening calling and shouting that hurt our ears. We had to follow behind, trampling through their shit and choking on their dust. Our eyes and nostrils were filthy with grit, however much we snorted.

'Can't tell us apart from the cattle,' Peter Long grumbled.

'Heading for the same place, most like,' John Thatcher said.

We came in by the East Gate. There was a crowd waiting to pay the tolls, and loud voices quarrelled over the cost. A salt wagon blocked the archway and a packhorse, over-laden with fleeces, was stuck behind it. The packhorse man cursed steadily, threatening the wagoner with hellfire if he didn't shift himself. The wagoner didn't care. He was a thickset man with bulging arms, a red face and a broken nose. We all had to wait. The sickly, heavy smell of the slaughterhouses and the reeking tanyards made the cattle restless and they snorted and pawed the ground so that the drovers had their work cut out keeping them together. And then we were through the bar and into the city.

I'd never seen anything like it, and I've never since seen a city to equal Chester as it was then, booming with trade because of the war. The streets were teeming with folk, and there were shops on either side – not just on one level but with rooms above – with arches, all built of stone. There was everything a body could wish for. There were bakehouses, a whole street of them, and the smell of fresh-baked bread had our bellies crying and would have had our mouths watering too, if they hadn't been dust dry. After that it was muddling but I remember butchers' stallboards and the carcasses, like so many hanged men, and having to duck our heads so we didn't bat into them. There were ironmongers, cobblers, cordwainers, glovers, vintners; there were skins and furs and woollen cloth. Smells of food wafted through the late afternoon: cooks, ready for business. I heard Gil Allbone groaning in agony.

'Look down there, men,' Peter Long smacked his lips. Below ground, in the undercrofts, were the taverns and we could see lucky men supping ale; this time our mouths did water. Street sellers bumped elbows with rich merchants and women in fine gowns brushed past us. Peter Long smacked his lips again and leered.

Nobody took any notice. Nobody stared at us marching down the main road of the town. They'd seen it all before.

'Eighteen hundred diggers. That's how many.' Bogo couldn't help himself. His mouth was streaming hot words, like the pisspot he was, bursting to tell us what he knew. 'Eighteen hundred, a month back, ready to march into Wales together with King Edward and his great army. They were all gathered here to topple the Welsh fool. Good riddance, I say. He should have bowed his knee and paid his dues long since.'

Dick Thatcher was right behind me. I heard him say, very quiet, 'Let it go, Dad.'

'He was in the right.' John Thatcher was growling, angrier than I'd ever heard him. 'The Prince was right to refuse. Pay homage? Bow his knee to that pard?'

'Dad, they'll hear you.'

'Let them hear!' But he lowered his voice all the same.

Bogo was full of himself. 'Master William and me, we were here as well, in the thick of it, while you lot were tucked up safe in the fens. There were three times more diggers than you lot. Think you're so special? You're the tail end, that's all.' He smirked in that way he had. 'Rat's tail end,' he added, and spat.

John Thatcher breathed in deep through his nostrils, like bulls did, but he kept his tongue still.

I was thinking, then, what they said in the village about John Thatcher. He'd been one of the barons' men, fighting against King Henry and his son Edward. Simon de Montfort was at their head; and with him the Welsh prince, Llewelyn, who was to marry de Montfort's daughter. At first, it all went well. They even had the King and his son caught and in prison but then Prince Edward, ever wily, escaped, and de Montfort was defeated and killed. They said Llewelyn would not bring his fighting men to England, and this is why de Montfort lost, but I don't know about that. What they said was that after the defeat, and with de Montfort dead, men went to hide in Ely but Longshanks drove them out and slaughtered whoever he could. John Thatcher came to our village with a half-grown son and a wife who died soon after. For grief, they said, for her slaughtered family. We sheltered him, of course. We sheltered most folk. We were freemen, not serfs, and we didn't think much to kings. Wasn't ours the abbey that had done for King John, years back?

We came to the Cross, where the roads met, and we turned down towards the river and the castle. We could hear the abbey bell ringing for Vespers and the jabber of Welsh, hard against Norman and Gascon, rough Saxon and polite Latin, and I knew Ned had heard it as well. His head went up and his beaky nose was sniffing out scents like a dog's; his flapping ears were listening for the voice of his Welshman with the red hair, but these men were fighting with the King, and against Llewelyn. Ieuan ap y Gof called them betrayers.

The boy could hear the murmur of voices. He strained to listen. Brother John and the Welshman. He relaxed a little. It didn't matter so much if Brother John caught him here. Ned might be with them and he'd promised Mam he wouldn't go back without Ned. The Welshman's voice was suddenly loud, right beside the door. The boy knew at once that Ned was not there and he himself must not be found. This was private talk.

'The longer I stay the more chance of being taken and the worse for the abbey. I must go, friend.'

'But the weather's bad for travelling and your leg's barely mended.'

'It took me to the smithy and back yesterday.'

'The smithy! You talk as if Dolforwyn were nothing more than a stride further.' A pause. 'Is it certain Dolforwyn is to be attacked?'

'Yes. Within weeks. Mortimer has his heart set on it.'

'Must it be war, Ieuan?'

'Edward's determined, and you know what that means. He never forgives and forgets, not Edward. He's had it in mind for years – since the barons had him locked up maybe.' The Welshman laughed. 'Well, it's nothing new. English kings have always made it their custom to invade us – it's a summer's outing for them. We know how to send them home again, in time for Advent.'

'Give your weather some credit for that, too.'

'Oh, I do, I do, Brother John – and the good Lord who makes it.'

'All the same, Ieuan, it's different this time. His army is huge. He has ships, weapons, trained men. Too many Welshmen have joined forces with him.'

'Traitors. Who can Llewelyn trust?'

'You; and men like you.'

'Yes, well – it's time this Welshman returned home. First light tomorrow, old friend.'

'And Gwydion?'

'He comes with me, of course. Where would I be without my nightingale?'

The boy was sidling away from the door. This was no place for him.

'And – Ned?' Brother John's voice was quiet, but the name stopped the boy dead. He didn't breathe. He waited.

'Ned? Why, Ned stays.' The Welshman's voice was light, surprised.

'He will be unhappy, Ieuan.' A longer pause.

'I know that.' Different, this time. Harsh, exasperated. 'But he must stay. There is no place for him where we are going and besides…' He stopped. His footsteps took him away from the door; the boy craned to hear. He thought he heard 'needed here', but maybe he was mistaken.

'You'll want food for your journey, and medicines.'

'Brother John, you are indeed a wonder and God has a place for you.'

The boy stayed as quiet as he could. It was war and the Welshman was leaving. He wondered which was worse.

We made camp in the castle bailey. Below the walls, the river Dee flowed fast to Bridgegate and the fisheries. Peter Long stood still and I swear I saw his nose twitch.

'Smell that?' he said. 'Smell that?' And he breathed in deep again. I breathed in with him and caught the smell; it was just like home.

'Eels.' He'd a broad grin stretched across his face. 'Guess what's for supper, lads?' He winked, but I couldn't laugh. It was like home, but not home. Same, but not the same. I didn't feel easy. Maybe it was the ghosts of the place. Everywhere there were signs of another army. The Romans, so they said. Chester was a Roman town, like Lincoln. The walls had been built up but it was clear they were very old. I shivered and was thinking about that army, set to march into Wales, just like us. I wondered if there had been a boy about my age, and if his life had shifted, like elf lights. I started to think, then, about war and how it went on and on. That didn't change. I slept badly. I dreamed of muddy water and everybody knows that means sorrow for the dreamer.

We had a day's grace. Master William told us we weren't leaving that day but the next. It started quiet enough, and there was a holiday feel about it. Rain had fallen and the sweltering air was sweeter. We were fed well, better than we were used to.

'Fatten us up,' John Thatcher said, 'like pigs in summer.'

Not long after that, Walter Reed took ill. He was pissing again and at first we took no heed. Stephen Fowler made some joke, true, but we took no heed of him either. We didn't much like him. He was one of those who had no good word for anybody. He'd said things about Ned until I longed to sink my teeth in his flesh. It was only Dick Thatcher who stopped me. It was Dick who heard the whimpering.

'Listen,' he said. He lifted a hand. We heard Walter Reed

plain then, whimpering like a child. It was Dick who carried him back to us, sat him down and wiped away the sweat beading his face. John Thatcher was fretful.

'Now, Walter, what's this then?'

'The stones, John, stones in my bladder. It's bad today.'

'Man, you've walked all this way and not said a word?'

Walter shrugged. I knew what he meant. What was there to say? We'd had the order so we marched. Nobody cared if we were in health or not. I was thinking about John Thatcher's sharp words and the way Cerdic Little had called him 'Water Rod', and all the time he'd hidden his pain. I wondered if John Thatcher was thinking of it, as well.

'You can't go tomorrow.'

'John, don't let them leave me behind. You mustn't leave me behind.'

'What can I do, Walter?'

'You know what they'll do to me.'

We well knew. There was a man in our village with the stones. Ned and me, we weren't supposed to see but we did. The man – it was Hubert Shakestaff – had his legs stretched wide and held tight. The healing man had his fingers up where no man's fingers should be. He had something, like a knife, and he cut into Hubert's arsehole. We saw blood spurt. Hubert was squealing like an autumn pig. The healing man had the stones out of him, though it laid him low for almost a fortnight.

'Not that, John, not that. I couldn't stand it.'

'But what else can we do?' John Thatcher sounded angry and I saw he was helpless.

'We can make the sign of the cross in his head. I've seen that done often.'

'Bleed him.'

'Sage, John. You know what they say: how can any man die when sage is growing in the garden?'

'Don't talk of dying, you halfwit.'

'What about the boy?' Dick Thatcher said. 'The boy carries simples. Brother John told me so. He knows their use.'

I jumped. The boy? Not me. He meant Ned.

The herbs were in raised beds walled with cut stone. Swallows chittered in the blue air, darting and diving about the abbey grounds and, out of sight, the river chuckled to the sea. The three of them walked with their shadows fastened to their feet, like souls. It was late summer and the herbs were ready to seed.

'*Lavandula spica*. Under Mercury. Gargle a decoction for toothache. It's good for pain in the head and the brain. And this is *Cannabis sativa*. Under Saturn. It will stop bleeding at the mouth and nose or anywhere. *Taxus baccata*. The tree of Saturn. See these berries? Death to anybody who eats them. Keep this in mind. *Alchemilla arvensis*...'

Brother John went on and on. The boy's head reeled. Was Ned really listening? Understanding? Remembering?

Ned stood quiet, looking down at Walter Reed. Dark hair, dark eyes, no silly grin. Just standing, not moving. Walter Reed was tight-mouthed, gritting his teeth against the pain. John Thatcher was pawing the ground and snorting like a horse.

'The boy can't help with this!'

'Think what he did with Squire Phillip's horse,' Gil Allbone said.

'He helped Godwin Salter when he had the toothache,' the Northman reminded us.

'Let him try,' Dick Thatcher said in his quiet way.

I said nothing. I watched. I could see what was bound to happen. Ned unfastened the bag that held the simples.

Lammas Eve. Brother John packing a bag with dried herbs, tinctures and salves. Ned, heron-slouched, hand jerking up to scratch an eyebrow.

'Understand, boy?'

Ned nodding his head and grinning his idiot grin.

'This is *Anthemis nobilis*. Under the Sun. It wonderfully breaks the stone.' Brother John stared at the phial containing its decoction; he was lost in thoughts that creased his face. 'Take care of this. It will be needed. And this. *Papaver somniferum*. Under the Moon. Dangerous in unskilled hands.' Brother John smiled. 'But not in yours, Ned, not in yours. God go with you.'

We left Walter Reed drowsing, at ease in poppy sleep. We came out into the bailey. Soldiers were horseshoe throwing, casting them over hilts of swords wedged into the turf. Welsh against Norman. We stood and watched a while. It didn't matter to us who won.

'Will? Will!'

My name, shouted loud over the game.

'Will. I knew you'd come here. I've been watching for you.'

It was Ralf. He had a scar down one cheek and a swagger in his walk. It seemed a long time since we'd waved him goodbye from the village.

'We're under orders to go with you tomorrow. We're your escort; your bodyguard to keep you safe from any Welsh dragons that might still be about.' He grinned then, looking more like Ralf. 'Will, it's good to see you.'

We clasped hands. We had been friends since childhood. We sat in the sun and swapped news. Ralf was full of the spring strike on Dolforwyn.

'We laid siege. Two weeks, Will, that's all it took. Last to be built and first to fall, that's what they're saying.' He laughed. He was full of being a soldier. 'Poor defences you see. He builds himself a brand new castle but fifty years out of date. Not even double-drum towers at the gateway. Didn't stand a chance against us. There was some fighting – that's when I got this.' He pointed to his cheek. He was proud of the mark. 'We had Master James of St George with us. They say he's coming up here soon. I doubt you've heard his name, though, eh Will?' Then he was looking at me sideways in a way I remembered, and my guts knotted.

'Remember that pretty boy who came with the music man last winter?'

'Music man?'

'The Welshman. He'd broken his leg and stayed at the abbey all winter.'

'Oh him, I'd forgotten.'

'I thought you and Ned were friendly with him?'

'Hardly. What about him?'

'His boy was taken prisoner. He said the Welshman was dead.'

I waited a heart's beat.

'What about the boy?'

'One of the Marcher lords liked his singing so he was taken into the household.' Ralf's voice held a sneer. He was back to being the soldier. 'He'll make a fine pet. There's others who'd have liked to make him sing a different tune. Or cut his tongue out. We want to know what happened to Ieuan ap y Gof.'

I waited another heart's beat.

'You said he was dead.'

'I said the boy told us he was dead.'

'You think he was lying?'

'To save his pretty skin? Maybe. We didn't find the body.'

'Does it matter?'

'Of course it matters. The man makes trouble. He uses his music to turn folk against the King. He knows how to work on them.'

Like a smith, I was thinking. Earth, water, fire, air. A ladybird was crawling up a blade of grass, bright red and black against turf dried to straw by the sun. A rattle of platters came from the kitchens and the smell of fish stew mingled with the horse smells from the stables. Someone was slicing bark from wood in the never-ending making of tent pegs. There was the clang of metal against metal and a shout went up. Norman cheers. The Welsh had lost, then.

'Will?'

'Yes?'

'It's better if they don't know he was at the abbey.'

'What do you mean?'

'Nobody knows who's fighting who. It's all arse over tit. It's bad enough John Thatcher being the barons' man. If they knew about the Welshman…' He flicked the blade of grass. The ladybird opened her wings and whirred away home. 'Take care, Will; these are dangerous times. It pays to be on the winning side. The Marcher lords know that. Besides, it's the King who's in the right of it. He has to protect his country against these rebels.'

A shapely girl with long dark hair walked out of the kitchens carrying a wicker basket piled with beans. Her glance slid across the two of us and Ralf grunted. 'Looker, isn't she?' He rolled over on his back and was laughing up at me. 'Had her last time we were here. It's another wench's turn tonight.'

I couldn't stop myself. 'What about Marie?'

'What about her? Not got dough in the oven, has she?'

'No.' I was thinking about Peter Long's wench and her swollen belly and swollen eyes.

'You're so young, Will. You've got it all to learn. I'll wed Marie, but I'll have some fun first. Reward for being a soldier, Will.'

I told him then how Marie was bullied by the village girls. It made him grin.

'Scrapping over me still, are they?'

I was almost glad when he had to go. I looked across at Ned. I wondered how much he'd taken in. I'd felt him stir at Ieuan ap y Gof's name but that was all.

'What are you thinking, Ned?' No answer. I didn't look for one. 'You heard what he said about Ieuan, didn't you? But nobody knows for sure what happened to him. There was no body found. He may be still alive.'

Alive. That was Ieuan. He was alive, like nobody else I have ever known, then or since. His red hair was alive, flaming. You could warm your hands at it. His eyes sparked life. I didn't wonder, then, why a *pencerdd*, a Welsh master poet, took so much interest in a village boy. I suppose I thought it was because this was Ned and Ned was clever. The white monks said so. I knew so. I loved him. At first because he stopped Mam belting me. Later, because he was good and gentle and everything was better because Ned was there. Later still, when I was older, because he was wise. Then the music man came and Ned was lost to me. I was jealous. I skulked and simmered. I hid round pillars. I tried to take Ned home to Mam and the girls. I told him he was a dimwit and the music man was nothing to him. Ned smiled his smile and gurgled and I think I knew, even then, he would stay with the music man to death.

Ned fingered the drilled holes in the length of the pipe. He rubbed along its smoothness then he raised it and started to play. It was the same song he'd played that February day, after the Welshman had gone beyond sight.

'Look out for him,' she warned, but how could he? His brother knew the way like a bat in the night, and he was blind. It was dark in the abbey where they had no right to be, let alone after Vespers on a winter's night. He wanted to shout,

'Wait for me!' like a child. He wanted to bawl. But he couldn't. He had to creep through the passages, silent as a worm in a tomb. At first, he thought the notes were drawn from his own soul, but it was music. Music such as he had never heard before. There must be a whole group of musicians playing for the Abbot. Ahead were lights and a hunched-heron shadow creeping closer and closer to a half-open door. 'Look out for him!' echoing in his ears but it was too late. The music stopped.

'Come out. I know you're there.'

A pause. A shift of sound. A whisper of strings in the air. Then the heron was in the doorway and the boy had to run to catch up with him. Candlelight sent shadows flickering into the corners of the room. Fire burned in the hearth. By it sat a small man in a high-backed chair.

'You have mice, Father Abbot,' said the man and he beckoned with the curved bow he held in his hand. 'Come closer.'

'Ned and Will,' Father Abbot sighed. 'Of course. Who else? Like the poor, always with us – and like mice, always finding a way in. Come, as Ieuan bids you. It's cold outside and we have a good fire in honour of our guest.' He smiled. 'And to ease his aching bones.'

The boy saw then that the man's left leg was strapped to wood and bound in soft linen. Ned had done as much for a kestrel with a broken wing, though without linen bandage.

'Well, what brings you this time?'

'Father Abbot, three of your sheep were wandering the marsh in the twilight, like lost souls, but we found them and brought them home again to you. Father Mark was grateful to us and let us warm ourselves by the fire before we went back over the marsh track in the dark. We—'

'I believe, young Will, you offered this tale last time you were here. Or was it the time before?'

The boy's tongue was stilled in his mouth, like the clapper of the abbey bell when it was muffled. Ned edged crabwise to the visitor. He touched the instrument and the strings quivered in the air. The boy wondered if it was possible that this had produced the sounds they had heard. It had sounded like a thousand voices but here was only one. It was an austere box of wood with a hump like a bridge over which four strings rested and two lay in free air. Compared with the harp or the lyre, this was as unadorned as the white monks' churches. The man considered them through eyes that were blue and limitless as the sky in summer.

'You like music? You would like to hear this *crwth* sing?'

Ned grinned. He touched the arc of bow, slid his finger along the horsehair.

The man laughed quietly. 'Well, Father Abbot, we have an audience of two mice.' He lifted the *crwth* and passed its leather strap about his neck. He adjusted the instrument so that it rested on his sternum, sideways to his body. The man's face became remote, serious, intent. His left arm curved to embrace the yoke, where the strings were splayed out before they disappeared into tunnels that led to the underside and the tuning pins. His fingers were long and pale, and the nails on that hand long. His bow arm was raised a moment then swept across the strings of the *crwth* and it breathed like a living soul yearning for eternity. The notes hussed endlessly, in harmony, as the sea on the shore, and then there were the higher notes, barely within hearing, plucked out of the air itself. Ned's eyes closed and his body folded around itself, as if the bow swept over him too and the sounds came from his soul.

'That is a very strange song to play in Edward's castle.'

A man in fine clothes stood in front of us. He was a head shorter than Ned – more my height so that I was looking straight into his eyes – but he had the stocky build of an ox and the smooth chin and long moustache of a Welshman. A Welsh ox stalled in an English stable. A second man stood next to him but I paid him no heed.

'Where did you learn that song, boy?' He was curt. Threatening. Horns lowered.

'Sir. I'm sorry, sir. He doesn't speak, sir.' My head was spinning, full of Ralf's warning and John Thatcher and where Ned had got that tune. I daren't tell him the white monks, as I'd told Guillaume, for fear he would get to know of their visitor. What kind of story could I whistle up? I shuffled my feet and kept my eyes down. I hoped he'd take it for shyness, a filthy village lad like me being spoken to by a great Lord like him. It felt like my guts were being wrung with red-hot pincers, like they say the devil does to damned souls.

'Doesn't speak? Or won't speak?'

'Can't speak, sir.'

'Then you speak for him, boy.'

'Yes, sir.' I was thinking. Hard. 'He's like a starling, sir.'

'A starling? What in the name of God…'

'Yes, sir. They listen to any sound, any song, and then they sing it themselves. That's what Ned's like, sir. He picks up anything. He could have heard the song anywhere.'

'That's true enough, Lord Hywel,' said the other man. 'I've heard it said he can play a psalm after only one hearing. It's a knack he has. Good with horses, too, wouldn't you say, boy?'

I looked up then and felt the first gladness since we'd heard the daybreak in Sherwood. Ned was already jerking his head and grinning. It was Squire Phillip.

'You know these two?' The ox man bellowed disbelief.

I could see his eyes, then: the whites and the brown rim and the black middle. I looked away.

'Indeed I do. They're our village boys come with Master William and the fossatores. Good boys, both.'

'This one is very young to be an expert fossatore. Master William was bringing experienced diggers?'

'The boy looks after his brother.'

'Hm. Simple, is he?'

'In a way,' Squire Phillip said smoothly. His look flicked over me and there was a warning in his eyes that made me bite back the words that said no. I knew then Ralf spoke true and I was frightened. Frightened for Ned, for John Thatcher; for Walter Reed in his white poppy sleep. This was a different danger, stalking and prowling us like the marsh devils, never quite in sight. You had to be cunning to fight a marsh devil. I stayed quiet.

Lord Hywel frowned. His voice was harsh. 'That song is forbidden. It is treason to play it. Understand?' I nodded. He frowned down on me still and I kept nodding, like a turtle dove, until he shifted so that he was no longer square in front of us. 'Squire Phillip, you'll attend to that other matter?' He had finished with us. The pincers slackened their grip.

'At once, Lord Hywel.'

But Squire Phillip loitered by us with a look on his face that made the pincers dig in again. Then he was smiling.

'I hear Ned's taken to physicking. If he deals with Walter Reed as well as he dealt with my sorry horse, the man has nothing to worry about.'

'You've seen him, Squire Phillip?'

'Yes. And Dick Thatcher. An excellent young man. He told me about your Ned and holds out great hopes that all will be well.' Squire Phillip made a purse of his lips. 'Had me promise we'd not leave Walter behind when we go tomorrow. Strange way to look after him I thought.'

I heard only the 'we'. 'You're coming with us?'

'Indeed I am.'

Two reasons to be thankful: a man who used a snaffle, not a curb; and a promise not to leave Walter behind.

'Like to see where we're heading tomorrow?' We nodded, the two of us speechless. 'Up here, then.' He led the way up to the blood red ramparts, saluting the soldiers at the top. 'With me,' he said to them shortly. I wasn't listening. I was staring out over marshland to the line of blue hills floating on the skyline. Two buzzards rested high on the air, mewing to each other. Below us the river rushed down to the fisheries and the wooden bridge we'd cross tomorrow, into the badlands just a bowshot away. The wharf was forested with masts; ships were being loaded. 'Shaped sandstone blocks from the Roman ruins outside St John's Church,' Squire Phillip said. 'Waste not, want not. It'll be shipped up river to where we'll build King Edward a fine new castle on the only solid rock in the area. How do you feel about that?'

'I'm not a mason.'

He laughed aloud. 'You're a fossatore, boy – a fledging fossatore, true, but a fossatore for all that. You're to dig foundations and ditches and the moat and banks for the new castle he's planning.' He added, to himself, not to me, 'Edward's Flint, and with it he means to set fire to all Wales.' He looked across at Ned, crouched like a cormorant on a rock.

'A remarkable lad, that brother of yours: he knows from Brother John how to physic; from Brother Mark how to whisper horses; and how to play Ieuan ap y Gof's own song as if he were the *pencerdd* himself. I wonder…what other gifts does he have?'

I had to lick my lips before I could answer; my mouth was dust dry, as if we were still on the road. I was thinking: *so this is why he asked us up here*. And after that: *but he already knows*. Brother John has told him. 'He knows languages. Latin and Norman.' A heart's beat. 'Welsh.'

'A dangerous combination, boy, in these times. Some people could get the wrong idea.' He shifted his gaze to mine. The young master was fair and just but he didn't stand any rubbish. 'I wouldn't want anyone to get the wrong idea. Take care.'

A third reason to be thankful: a fair and honest man.

'I'll look out for him, sir.'

His face softened. 'You're a good boy, Will.' I gawped, both for what he said and because I didn't think he even knew my name. Then I was thinking of the pisspot who wasn't a pisspot but a Gascon who said I was a good boy, like his own son, and I wondered how it could be true. Mam always said I was as much bother as Dad, and he was bound for hellfire.

Squire Phillip turned to lead the way back down the steps then turned back again. 'Master Richard of Chester is in charge of the building works at Flint. They call him the Engineer.' He stared away, across the blue hills. 'He also leases the fisheries and mills on the Dee – yes – the ones you can see by the bridge. He's a clever man, and not one for fools. Best make sure your friend Long knows that before he goes fishing for his supper.' He was away down the steps while my jaw was still dropping.

John Thatcher looked for me that evening. John Thatcher never spoke a word to me, unless he had to – or wanted to sneer.

'Your brother did well today.' It was like grinding corn from sluggish millstones. 'The third dose has made a difference. That and the music he plays for Walter.'

'That's good,' I said. He seemed to want an answer.

'Yesterday, boy.' I waited. 'Yesterday, at the smithy, he gave the sergeant a pipe he'd made. Why was that? Not for his blue eyes, that's for sure.' He laughed at his own joke but it was false.

'The sergeant spoke kindly to me. Ned wanted to thank the man. That's all.'

'Oh?' He didn't say anything to that and I was glad. I said nothing about the son who was my age and the woman who was his wife. 'Didn't the sergeant ask where Ned learned to play the pipe so well?'

'Yes.'

'Oh?'

I was worn out with worry and was thinking marsh devils would be easier than this. 'I'm not so dull in my wits, John Thatcher, and neither is Ned. I said nothing about the Welshman. And it's not us who were barons' men.' I was bristling at him, getting my fists ready.

'Don't try your temper on me, you young whelp.'

'Let the boy be, Dad. He's no fool.'

'Maybe not, Dick, but there's none of us above suspicion. Dangerous times and a dangerous King.'

Three warnings. I dreamed for a second time of muddy water.

✝ Let me build up that fire again, get it crackling. Blue flames – hoar frost tonight, for sure. You're wondering why I didn't tell you from the start Ned was so learned. I promised you not one word a lie, but not where the words would fall. Twists and turns, that's what I warned. Habit, maybe, after all those years of looking out for him. And the times we lived through were dangerous. What you knew was best kept to yourself. You're too young to remember how it felt. That was the summer Edward gathered all England, half Gascony and most of Wales against the Prince. King Edward had power at his fingertips, even if he had to hold out his hand to Lucca to bankroll his kingdom, and he wanted to use it. Dafydd was with him then, and Eleanor, de Montfort's daughter; a prisoner though Edward called her his guest. He made plans. How he made plans. He studied his Tacitus inside out, did Edward. We should have known he'd leave nothing to chance but we didn't think until it was too late.

There. That's blazing well enough for the fires of hell. I've not told you everything about Ned, and I'll not tell you now. Keep you guessing, though they say confession's good for the soul. Maybe you'll guess right before I've done. Maybe I'll never tell – keep the secret safe in my shroud, hey?

Listen.

We were marching through a dead land. No sound, except the noises we made: metal jingling, leather creaking, hounds panting; a horse snickering and silenced. Our feet, tramping mile after mile after mile through a dead land. No dream. No nightmare. This was real.

Where were the faces with staring eyes, shouting out stems and leaves from their mouths. The lichen like shaggy hair. Bird song at break of day in the great forest.

As far as we could see in front, and as far behind, the forest was cut down. To right and left, a bowshot wide: cut down. From Chester to where the new castle would be, twenty miles, and for four hundred feet across: cut down. That's what they said. I wasn't the one who knew about numbers. All I knew was that we were marching through a gaping stretch of dead land, on and on, where a forest should be, and living things.

Church walls show us hell. The priests warn us how it will be. Tales for bairns and silly folk. I've seen hell here on this earth and it's nothing like they say. Nothing. Hell is desolation. That dead land was the start.

'It's your safe conduct,' Ralf said, though I saw he was ill at ease. Not so much the brave soldier today. 'It's to stop Llewelyn's men from ambushing us. Edward had a thousand woodcutters on the job. Talk about hard work. I had to do my share of hefting the tree trunks to the carts following behind us. You'll find the timber's stacked at Flint, ready for the palisades.'

No sound of birds. No rustle in the undergrowth. No coppiced wych elm. No birch barks gleaming in the sun. No tangle of brambles with fruit almost ripe for eating. No oak trees. Only slashed and burned stumps. Sometimes, there were heaps of branches hacked from the bodies of the trees. Twigs trampled under our feet, crunched under hooves.

'Like I said,' Bogo gloated, 'the work's been done. Riding on the tail of the fighting men, that's what you're doing.'

All of us silent; all of us keeping our thinking to ourselves. The weather had turned around. Drizzle fell from a sky as white as a blind man's eye.

'A song, Ned?' Dick said, after midday. 'Keep us in spirit?'

Ned shook his head. Dick didn't ask a second time. That day, the swan pipe was as silent as the dead land and the men marching through it.

Four

The pebble is pale and smooth as an egg. It nestles in your warm palm, tucked in the hollow between thumb and fingers. It is cool and hard. Rest it there a moment. Cold pebble in warm hand: soft flesh on hard stone. Let it drop. The plash into quiet water startles the silence. A small circle eddies out. Clusters of waves ripple into larger circles, and larger still until they are exhausted and die and the water is quiet again. This is how we hear, fainter and fainter the further we are from the source.

We heard the camp before we saw it. Spades slapping and sucking on turf and wet mud. Crack of wood on wood, dead as gallows. Rattle of hand barrows. Then the stench: human, animal – who could tell? We were choked by it. We could see the camp now through drizzle that turned late day to gloom. The one solid spit of land for miles around: a dull brown hillock poking its dirty nose above empty marshland. To the south it was backed by crouching hills and to the north fronted by a doorstep of muddy water. The water stretched so wide we couldn't see the far bank that dismal afternoon, though we'd been told it was the same river that ran past Chester. East and west ran marshland, disappearing into the mist and rain.

'Dear God,' somebody muttered.

'Like flies on a dung heap,' John Thatcher said, but even he sounded winded.

'Eighteen hundred bodies have to shit somewhere,' said Bogo. It didn't bother him. 'That's how many we are at Flint camp.'

Eighteen hundred. I hadn't thought there were three hundred of us living cheek by jowl in the fens. Chester didn't hold so many souls. Eighteen hundred blowflies crawling over clay brown as turds. Smoke rose and sank on the air, and white ash fell with the rain.

We sat around the fires that evening, huddled together for comfort and warmth, and listened to the men. This was a gathering place and a leaving place. You never knew who would be gone when you woke in the morning. Men came. Men went. And all left their shit.

'Digging cesspits. That was my first job.'

'Me, digging banks and ditches. The King's giving a bonus to the best workers.'

'And a curse for the worst!' They laughed but it was true; no backsliding allowed here, no bad workmanship, however you slithered about in mud.

'Mind you, having the Welsh in bowshot keeps us digging fast enough.'

'We've got them on the run, now. Edward's rounding them up.'

'He should wipe them out while he has the chance.'

'Even so, thank God the palisades go up tomorrow. We might sleep easy yet.'

Palisades: wood from the dead forest, just as Ralf had said. The fire breathed woodsmoke; pale ash fell through blackened stumps to the red heart.

'Where do you come from?' Dick asked.

Yorkshire. Norfolk. Suffolk. Northumberland.

The Great Fens, we said.

So many, so far. They talked of home, of wives, of bairns left behind. Edward's great army: men longing to go home. When was it Ned took up the pipe? He played for every man there: sounds of home, of longing; peace, not war; summer flowers, not stench of shit. Above us, beyond banks of rain cloud, we caught glimpses of the night sky and the stars.

'Young un's worn out,' I heard someone say, but from far off.

'It's not right,' said a rough-edged Yorkshire man. 'This is no place for bairns. Even the smiths' boys aren't as young as him.'

I slept but I dreamed of muddy waters, and three times dreamed is true.

That first week the muddy water was real enough; after a summer of sun, rain set in as if to spite us all. The earth churned to thick, clogging mud that we had to dig and cart and pile, heap on heap, to build the banks and ditches for the town. Town, not camp; it was like nothing we had seen before. No motte, no bailey. The town was laid out square, like the sieve Mam kept hanging up by the hearth.

'An experiment,' Squire Phillip told us in the quiet of early morning. We crouched under a canvas shelter. Rainwater dripped from its lip and splashed into puddles of mud. 'They say the King has seen such places – in France or on his travels. He plans a town and a castle, and burgages to rent for those who choose to live here when we've won the war.'

'They'll be trampled in the hurry to get here,' John Thatcher said.

So we kept on digging down through yellowy gravel and further down through brown silt, digging like the wriggling worms we unearthed with every spadeful. We dug down for ten full feet. We ferried barrows of stiff clay and hard-packed it over the outer slope for a covering. We hefted the gravel over to build the second of the banks and heaped it up. Not as high as the outer bank, but still huge. We dug into flaking, crumbling sandstone that was blue and grey and yellowy green. We scraped black shale. We burnt acres of brushwood. Palisades ran proud around the top of the four inner banks, and the gateways were solid against attack.

'See,' Ralf said. 'If they're daft enough to attack, they've got to get up the first bank and then down into the ditch. Then they've still got a second bank to go, and they won't stand a chance. That's a fifty-foot wide killing field down there. We'd just pick 'em off with short bows.' He was grinning, thinking about it; all but licking his chops.

Master William led us fen men to the river. Here was where the castle would be built, separate from the town: four square, with round towers at each corner. Except – and at first we didn't know what to think – the fourth tower was to be bigger than the rest, and ringed by its own moat. We were to dig the outer moat first. Not so easy: every day we grappled with the tide, and we'd never seen tides like it.

'You watch yourselves,' Giles from Yorkshire warned us.

'It comes racing in across the sands. It can cut you off. Leave you stranded beyond deep water. You've not a hope, if that happens. It's over thirty feet high at spring tides. Not like our sea at all.'

No, not like our grey northern sea, nor was there any sound of it; only the lap and suck of river water. At low tide there was sand and mudflats stretching across to England, looking as close as if we could paddle across. There was a ford over the sands when the tide was low, but it was dangerous.

'And that's the way the King arrived in July, riding across the ford as if he was travelling his own highway. There's kingship for you! What a leader.'

One of the veterans told us that. We didn't say much in answer. John Thatcher started to mutter something about King John and the Wash but Peter Long kicked him, hard from the way John Thatcher grunted. So we looked and looked at the marshland and watched the way the water whirled and eddied with undertow and listened to the birds chittering a warning and it was the same, and not the same.

We feared the serpents that lurked in the mud. We feared the sand that looked so quiet but under it were monsters that would drag you down. We feared the dragons that folk said lived in this land, with their flaming breath and creeping legs and leathery wings.

Fear or not, Peter Long couldn't rest till he'd got himself a handful of the mullet that were swarming in the shallows. When he gutted them, their bellies were full of mud and their flesh was foul.

There was no thinking. Just doing. Arms and legs aching. Shoulders stretched. Throat parched. Head splitting. Do the job right and get paid. Get it wrong, lose pay. And be put on the worst jobs. We were clay men, coated with red-brown mud that dried to a crust in the wind and dribbled down our bodies in the rain. For days we couldn't see the far bank for the rain and mist. Sometimes, with the wind northerly, we heard the noise of quarrying on the Wirral bank. Ten thousand stones, they said, were coming from Shotwick. We lived by numbers at that time. Mostly the wind blew from the west, wet and cold. It seemed to us the seasons had halted. It could have been summer or autumn or winter or spring, though it was barely weeks since we had come to the camp, weeks since we had left the Fens. It seemed a lifetime away. Now ours was a world of dark, heavy earth and rot and back-breaking digging.

It was only after work, when we hugged the fireside, that the world seemed right.

Firelight flickering in the hearth and the smell of Mam's broth. The roof fresh-thatched with reeds. Home made safe against winter storms. Folk you knew living close by.

There were talk and tales and Ned's playing and they drove away the day's mud and rain, easing our aching bodies and our souls. At other campfires, there were sharp squabbles and wrangling that sometimes came to fists. Not at ours. We looked out for each other, and where folk look out for each other, there is peace. That is when I told my first stories, of Ned and me. I told of the time we sneaked apples, with Ralf, and they laughed, because they knew Ralf and his ways; I told of the time I fell in the deep pond and how Ned pulled me out; I told of the carved heads in the church, and who they were, and even John Thatcher laughed to hear it. It was the same and not the same as telling tales to get us out of the mire. I didn't tell about the Welshman. It was then Dafydd Gwyn told us of St Winifrede, Tewyth's daughter, whose Welsh name is Gwenfrewi. The Prince Caradog of Hawarden lusted for her but she refused him and he hacked off her head in a rage. We had heard the tale before, Ned and me—

'Her head sheared from her shoulders and, lapped in shining hair, rolled to the bank's edge, turning and turning. And her eyes, her eyes of immortal brightness, round and round they came and flashed towards heaven.'

The Welshman's voice held the boy in a spell. He sat still as the carved saints in their niches. Then the sweep of the bow across the strings of the *crwth*, and its sound shivered through his whole body. Gwydion the beautiful took up the story in an *englyn*. No sulking now, no glowering glances, but a voice that resonated with the *crwth*, but was separate from it. The world wrapped itself around the room, around the listeners, the players, and there was nothing except the song itself.

'*Her precious blood spilt on stone and moss.*
Forever and forever
the sweet smell of frankincense and violets
shall rise from where her blood was shed.'

Dafydd had us all with our mouths gaping and ears wagging. He knew how to tell a tale and when to wait and where to drop his voice to a whisper.

'The head rolled on and came to rest inside the church door. Her uncle, St Beuno, took up the head and placed it back on her body. He blew air into the mouth and nostrils. He prayed, and she came back to life. And, out of the ground where her head had lain, burst sweet water that gushed in a never-ending stream down the hillside to Basingwerk and out into the Dee, as it does to this day.

'Cursed be Caradoc.
The earth shall open and swallow him.

'And the water is so pure and clear and has such healing in it that many make a pilgrimage there,' Dafydd said. 'They come for the stone, palsy, the cough; the lepers and cripples come; women who are barren; old men covered in running sores: all who ail come here. And as sure as the seasons turn, they recover and revive and bless her name.' He poked the fire with a stout branch, scattering sparks into the air. 'Or they used to make pilgrimage here, before this cursed war.

'And those who ask for her help
shall receive it;
if not at the first,
not at the second,
then at the third time of asking.
Blessed is St Winifrede.'

What none of us reckoned on was Walter. His pains had eased but he was no longer Walter Greed, snaffling more food than the next man. He was thinner than ever but fast mending.

Word got round and next we knew there was a stream of men at our billet, all wanting to see what Ned could do for their aches and pains. It started with a man who had gut ache. Then a man with head pains. A man with the cough and hot shivers. Ned's bag of salves and tinctures was emptying fast and there were more men every day. Then Bogo came, daring us to snigger. None of us did. He'd a gash on his arm from a cutting tool and it was angry red. Ned bound it with a salve of *Lysimachia nummularia*, and gave him a drink of the same.

One morning, it all shifted. I'd been set to bundling twigs and binding them with withies to make hand brooms. I was thinking it was to keep me from under their feet because I was too skinny and worn out to keep up with the digging. I wished I could be a smith's boy and keep warm by the furnace. Peter Long shouted to me to fetch a jug of water. I took the jug down to where they were, and a new-made broom to show. Next I knew there was loud yelling and a hefty clout in the small of my back that sent me spinning through air and into the muddy water. I closed my mouth too late and gulped the foul stuff. I clawed to the surface, gasping and heaving.

Wet clay clogged my ears and my nostrils. I thought I was dead. I thought the ugly things under the mud would come and get me. I kicked out and screeched and there was a face turned towards me. It was the Northman, his mouth shut tight, and I screeched again and the muddy water filled my mouth with a second tide. So this is what it's like, Northman. Then hands reached down to haul me out but it was my brother's hand that caught me, my brother's arms twining round me, sucking me up from the red-brown mud and holding me tight. I was retching and shivering and I'd lost a boot and there was no hope of getting it back. The jug was shattered and lost. The new broom was sunk out of sight. It was Harold Edmundson who'd knocked me flying to save my life. He hauled himself on to the bank beside me, on hands and knees, coughing up gobbets of mud. Lodged in the mud under the water was a hulk of timber ten-feet long. It had tumbled from the earthworks above us. It missed my head by a hand's breadth. I was thinking of my muddy dreams even while I was shivering and shaking. I don't know what Harold Edmundson was thinking. He slapped me on the shoulder, later, when we were warm and dry, and said something in his own tongue.

The day after that Ned and me went with the turf cutters out on the marshes. Ned was to gather what herbs and plants he could use and I had a bucket pushed in my hand. 'Bring back berries,' they said. 'Don't come back till it's full.' That was the day we woke to sun and blue sky and clouds sitting heavy on the far bank. It was steaming hot and the flies were biting. I felt pity for the men who had to dig the day away. We had been here since the beginning of August and now it was but mid September but the work went on and on and we longed for the time we could go home. At least, when winter came, the work would stop.

We stayed out till the light was fading. I had a bucket full of samphire and sea holly, both with parts good for eating, and rosehips and early blackberries. Ned had a harvest of rushes that the white monks called *Juncus*. Boiled in water, the roots help the cough, and there were many with the cough, what with the water and rain and the wind in the west.

Three days after that, King Edward arrived.

'Come to breathe new life into his clay men,' John Thatcher scoffed. If it was blasphemy, nobody said.

It was the first time I'd seen the King, though I'd heard tell of him from the moment I was born. They called him Longshanks and long shanks he had. He was head and shoulders above the rest and it gave him a kingly look. His head was just like it was on the new pennies. A vain man, Edward, and he'd had coins minted with his likeness stamped on them. He was like the coins except for his eyes. Eyes show the soul. That's what they say. Edward's eyes were empty. They went through you, like a war sword through flesh. And there was that right eye, with its drooping lid. I felt myself shrinking and hoping I never had to meet those eyes. He came on a pale horse with his hounds and hunting birds that he loved so much. He'd had prayers offered and candles lit when one of his birds was sickly. That's what they said. I was thinking he cared more for his birds and beasts than for men.

Then I was thinking about his other name. The one we spoke when we knew we could not be heard.

The lion roared as if it were alive. Its long tail looped over its back and swished across the page against a background of red and blue squares. The boy traced the shape with careful fingers. Further down the page, another lion was at bay, attacked by three ravenous creatures. The boy wondered if the lion would throw them off his back and pounce on them and devour them, as they deserved. Brother John turned the heavy parchment of the Bestiary. There was a heron, shoulders hunched. The boy nudged his tall brother.

'Look, Ned.'

Brother John smiled. 'A bird wise above all others,' he said.

The next page held a letter O that was made with burnished gold and framed in a blue square patterned with curving sprays. It was spoilt by faulty lines. Brother John sighed and smoothed the parchment. 'So easy to make the wrong choice. The monk who did this failed to be guided by the pricking. See here? And here?' He pointed to a tiny splatter of blue. 'Well, it is still a precious book and we are lucky to have it. Perhaps it is the more beautiful because it is flawed.'

He turned the page again. Black bean shapes with legs laboured across a brown hillock. Ants.

'They act in unity. If men are sensible, like these ants, they will be rewarded.'

'Brother John?'

'Yes, child?'

'Brother John, why do they call the new King the Leopard?'

An intake of breath. The boy held his own breath and wondered if he would be punished. He didn't know why. He had heard the men talk of the Leopard, and there had been laughter.

'Where have you heard this?'

'Everybody says so.'

'Well, better not repeat it. The king is a proud man. He would be angry. The leopard is the offspring of the mating of a lion and a pard.'

'But the lion is the king of the beasts.'

'And the pard is a deadly beast that kills with a single leap.'

The page showed green grass, a deer peacefully grazing,

unaware of the dangerous beast springing towards him that very second. The boy shivered, felt teeth sink into flesh, felt the quiver of the gentle deer as it sank on its haunches, the leopard feasting on the still living body.

'The leopard's coat, child, is spotted with evil.' Brother John took the boy's chin between his thumb and forefinger. 'Look at me, child.' The boy was wary. 'Sometimes, Will, it is better to hold your tongue. Bite it, if needs be. Better to keep the words in, if talking can only bring harm.'

'Like calling the King a leopard?'

'Yes. Like that.'

It was later, much later, that he realised Brother John had not denied it: the King was a leopard.

'Is he staying at the camp?' I asked.

'Don't be a halfwit. Of course he isn't. He'll make himself very comfortable thank you over at Basingwerk Abbey. All English monks there, no Welsh.'

'I hear they have fine, fat sheep on the salt marsh.' That was Peter Long.

'That they have. Fine, fat and tasty, I reckon.' That was Godfrey from Northumberland. From the first day, they'd been friends. Marrers, Godfrey called them.

The King stayed at the abbey for near a week. He came almost daily to the workings where he was often deep in talk with Richard the Engineer. He didn't seem to mind the stench or the rain or the mud, any more than he minded the men. We might as well have been worms. His care was only for the work and that it was going ahead as he wanted. He ordered a shift in the digging of the outer moat. We groaned, thinking of aching arms and blistered hands and wasted struggle. Then we woke one morning to find that a good many fossatores had gone; four smiths and four of their boys, half of the charcoal burners and some of our fighting men. Ralf was one of them.

'To Rhuddlan, with the King,' Squire Phillip said.

'Oh yes? They'll be digging ditches for him there, will they?' John Thatcher said.

'Happen a new castle as well,' somebody joked, 'now motte and baileys are out of favour.'

Squire Phillip didn't laugh. 'Yes,' he said. 'That's what most of you will be doing, before winter sets in. Not just a new castle, men. King Edward plans a new course for the river. This will be a great undertaking. No king has made plans like this. Master James of St George is expected daily.'

'No going home for us, then,' said a Yorkshireman, 'not this side of Michaelmas.'

'Happen not then. I've heard we'll be working through winter,' said Thomas Wytheberd.

'Never. That's never been done before.'

'There's a deal that's never been done before, man. We're living in new times.'

That was the day Peter Long and Godfrey from Northumberland wangled a trip turf cutting and came back with the carcass of a fine, fat sheep. They hid it in a cart but how they kept it from the soldiers on guard, they wouldn't say.

'No one will smell it roasting,' they said, 'with this stench around us.' Daft, we thought. We were all so used to the smell of shit anything else was bound to be noted. 'It's for Walter,' they said. 'Perk him up.'

Perk him up? The whole camp was alive with it. This was roast meat, spitted over a fire, not grain porridge or bean stew. It wasn't finished cooking before we had Bogo and the rest down on us and we bought them off with a promise of roast flesh. It made no difference. The next day we heard that Peter Long and Godfrey Northumberland had been taken before Master William and Squire Phillip and charged with stealing abbey sheep, and that carried a worse punishment than stealing two sticks of eels. Lucky for them that Richard the Engineer had gone to Rhuddlan as well. It was his voice that usually gave judgement and he was a harsh man. Even so, no one spoke that morning and the air was heavy. We crept up to the place where they were kept, Ned and me, and it was dark and stinking, too small for one man, let alone two. I whispered to them and Peter Long whispered back. He wanted to know their punishment but none of us knew.

Ned poked his sharp elbow into my side and we shadowed through the camp to Master William's tent. Squire Phillip was with him; we could hear him plain through the canvas.

'They are two good workers,' Squire Phillip was saying. 'Too good to lose. They know how to slant a spade. They've an eye for angles. Peter Long is well liked. He tells a good tale; he keeps the men laughing and in good heart.'

'And if every popular man escaped justice, what would become of law and order? What sort of society would we have then, Squire Phillip?'

'Of course you're right, sir, in the normal way but…'

'Yes?'

'These are not normal times, sir. The men miss their homes;

they are living in filth and danger.'

'What of it? They're paid well and fed well, though it might not be on the Abbot's sheep.'

'They are close knit, sir. They wouldn't like it.'

'You mean a rebellion? We've men-at-arms who'd deal with that. We must make an example of thieves.'

Silence. We pressed closer.

'Sir. Have you seen how there's no fighting in that camp? The men look after each other – and then there's the boy.'

'Ah yes. The boy.' Master William's voice changed. Was it less harsh? 'A strange boy, that one, who can charm music out of the air. Oh, don't look surprised, Squire Phillip. I travelled with them from Lincoln, remember. Now he's acting as camp physician, from what I hear. That oaf Bogo was singing his praises. And the younger one; took a ducking, so I heard.'

'Yes, sir. Harold Edmundson saved him. The men like him. They say he's got courage.'

'Who authorised them to go out with the turf-cutters?'

'I did, sir.' Squire Phillip said it quiet but he didn't sound sorry. 'The boy needed a rest. He was half drowned and scared out of his wits. Besides, it's backbreaking work for the men, let alone a skinny little whelp like him. And Ned's running out of herbs.'

'Pampering, Squire Phillip, does no good.'

'No, sir.'

'But it was well done, in this case.'

'Thank you, sir.'

'Running out, you say?'

'Yes, sir.'

'That would be a pity. We need every man healthy, here, no

shirking.'

'Yes, sir. I was wondering, sir…' He was careful.

Master William was sharp. 'Yes, Squire Phillip?'

'Well, sir, I wondered if the Abbey would let us have fresh supplies.'

'Did you now? First our men steal abbey sheep and then we demand their medicines?'

'It's for the war effort, sir. The Abbot would be glad to give what help he could to the King.' Another silence. That careful note again. 'Need the Abbot know about the sheep, sir?'

'Squire Phillip. What exactly are you suggesting?'

'Just that we keep it within this camp, sir. Of course, the two men must be punished but—'

'—they are good workers who know how to slant a spade.' Master William was withering. 'Squire Phillip, I am not the authority here. You know that.'

'But you are listened to, sir.'

Master William was tap, tap, tapping his fingers on wood.

'Why are you so concerned, Squire Phillip, for these thieving rats?'

'They are men, sir, and Peter Long is my father's villager.'

Tap, tap, tapping. When he spoke, his voice was final: 'Give them a beating and a warning that there's no second chance. Any more and they'll have no hands to dig with.'

'Yes, sir. Thank you, sir. And the supplies?'

'I'll speak to the Abbot myself. No promises, Squire Phillip, no promises.'

'No, sir. Thank you, sir.'

'Well, what are you waiting for? You've work to do.'

We clung close to the edge of the tent. Squire Phillip walked out and away and then, without warning, he stopped and turned about. And saw us. He beckoned us to him.

'Ears on legs. I should have known. Heard it all, I suppose?'

'A beating, and simples for Ned.' I wanted to thank him but I didn't know how. I couldn't even smile. I caught his hand and kissed it. He pulled it away, out of reach, but not in anger.

'That's enough of that, young Will. I hope Peter and Godfrey will be as grateful after a beating. And no promise of simples, mind.'

'No sir.' I waited. Ned was speaking fast, more of a slur than ever, so I had to listen hard. 'Sir, he asks if he can have holy water from St Winifrede's well.'

Squire Phillip threw back his head and laughed aloud, and it was a good thing to hear in that dreary place, though I didn't know what I'd said to make him laugh. It brought Master William to the opening of his tent. He looked ready to swoop.

'Holy water from the well, Master William: that's what they're demanding. And I suspect a list of simples as long as King Edward's battle sword.'

Master William looked us over, his face more kestrel than ever, and I wanted to flinch away but I didn't. I had courage. That's what they said.

'Holy water?'

'Yes, sir.' I kept my head up and forced myself to look into his straight, hard gaze. 'And Ned wants to go to the well himself to see it.'

Five

Listen to the gentle melody. Sink into its mild and quiet slumber. Let peace lap around you. Then rouse yourself. Purge yourself of stupor. Let your heart beat faster and your mind wake up. Let pitches and ratios join with melody. A sweet tune delights infants, but a harsh one spoils the pleasures of listening. Mourners in tears turn their lamentations to music. Sweetness is summoned from the soul and fury and wrath are expelled.

Chill morning, and the wetness of autumn mist heavy on man and beast alike. The camp was behind us, and the air smelt fresh, blowing off the crouching hills. The mist was shifting, and the sky was hued with pink and pale blue and stippled with cloud. Flocks of geese were arriving for winter, just like they did at home. We could barely see them but we heard their wings creaking and their noisy honking. Terns were warbling their warning and curlews were piping. It was the day the first rafts were coming across the river with their loads of timber. More than a hundred, that's what they said. Some said two hundred, all told.

'More timber,' John Thatcher grumbled. 'We'll be buried in timber before we're done.'

But Ned and me, we wouldn't be there to see it. We were going to fetch holy water from St Winifrede's well. Days had passed. Peter and Godfrey were a sorry sight still for the beating was thorough. They had to be a warning to us all.

'Better than having our hands tucked in our belts,' Godfrey said, 'and us harmless, like.'

'Better than having our eyeballs food for fish.'

They looked at each other. They could laugh now. 'Still got our tackle, lads. Just wanting the chance to use it.'

But they groaned in the night. I heard them. And they were glad of whatever comfort Ned could give them. Even so, they were alive and whole and the heaviness was gone from the camp. Men put their backs into the work, as men do for masters who are fair and just.

Then the Abbot gave us leave to go to the well. Squire Phillip told us the news. 'And I'm to go with you – make sure you keep out of mischief.' His look was light, and I thought he was as glad as we were to be out of the camp, if only for a day. We had two soldiers with us, and we were all on horseback.

Ned was astride a dull-looking nag, his long legs dangling past her belly. His eyes were shining bright and he was grinning and gurgling to her and she was livening up and snorting back at him. I was perched in front of one of the men-at-arms. It was Sion Sais, a Welshman who spoke bad English, though he'd an English father. He picked me up and slung me across his horse as if I was nothing but a bag of corn, and I sat slumped like one, too frightened to move. I'd never been astride a nag before. I didn't know it would feel so high up, or so stumbling. I wanted to laugh and pinch myself – two village lads carried on horseback with two soldiers to guard us and Squire Phillip to lead us. It didn't seem real. The nag settled into a jogging trot that had me jerking up and down in agony until I let myself fall and rise with it. We went along the marsh track towards the abbey.

'The Abbot wants to see you both,' Squire Phillip said. 'It's an honour so best behaviour. No glowering, Will. Keep yourself still, Ned.' He stopped, looked at me. 'Remember what I said at Chester, Will?'

I nodded. Suddenly, my heart felt cold and my chest was fearful. I was forgetting Chester. I thought of something.

'Sir, will he ask us about the herbs?'

'Maybe. Why?'

'We only know the Latin names, sir.'

'"We," young Will?'

I was red in the face. 'Yes, sir.'

'Hiding your light under a bushel, Will?'

'I don't know what you mean, sir.'

'Never mind. But you're right; try not to use the Latin. Can't Ned just point, for the good Lord's sake?'

'If we're in the garden, sir. But it might be the physic room, and then it's all salves and tinctures and ointments and names.'

Squire Phillip thought about that. I wondered, then, what he knew. He knew about his men. About his acreage. But what did he know about us, the little people? We were two village boys, that was all. Then I was thinking about the white brothers, and how Ned had the run of the abbey and nobody cared. It was then I began to wonder why the white brothers didn't shut him out, and if Mam truly knew where he was. I wondered if Mam ever knew about the music man. She never asked where we'd been, and that wasn't like Mam.

The moon had risen long since and they were late, later than they had ever been, coming home across the abbey fields and skirting the edges of the fen before taking the track that led to the village. An owl swooped past on silent wings. Somewhere, a fox barked and little things skittered. The sky was stuffed full with stars, like a feast cake. The boy was practising his story, the one that would keep them out of trouble. Ned was grinning and gurgling and prancing alongside him, happy because the evening had been good, and he had learned new songs, and the music man had praised him.

Their cottage was dark but for one candle. Mam was waiting, then. He opened the door. 'Mam?' he called. No answer. She was there, though, hunched in a chair staring into the embers of the fire. 'Mam, I've found him. I've brought him back. He—'

She turned her head. Her face was set like a two-day-old pudding.

'You'll both be wanting your supper, I dare say.'

'Ay, Mam.' For once, his tongue froze, and the words as well. She wasn't shouting angry, and she didn't clout him, but she moved like an old woman, and her fingers fumbled the ladle and the bowls. He kept silent though he didn't know why. Ned was smiling, smiling, and Mam's gaze settled on him and her eyes were pools as deep as any in the fens.

'Do you mean Ned can read?'

'Yes, sir. Some things.'

'In Latin, Welsh and Norman, I suppose?'

'Just Latin, sir.'

'Yes, of course. I should have known.' It took me a while to know he was joking. 'Well, we'll have to meet that when we get there.' His head went up in the old way, as I'd seen him back in the village. He was the young squire again, handsome and smiling and happy in the bright autumn sunshine. 'We've a grand day for it, Will. It's good to be out of the muck for a while.'

'Isn't it dangerous, sir?'

'Maybe, but it's on abbey land and we've a brave pair of lads with us. Don't let worry spoil the day, Will. There'll be enough to worry about when we get back.' His face shadowed and his lips were tight and I knew then that he didn't want to be here, any more than the rest of us. He spoke to the Welshman. 'All right with him up in front of you, Sion?'

'Like a feather, Squire Phillip, like a feather.'

'A sack of feathers, maybe.' Squire Phillip grinned, like a boy grins, and I found myself grinning back, and Sion as well. Then the walls of Basingwerk came in sight.

The boy stayed as quiet as he could. It was war and the Welshman was leaving. He wondered which was worse.

'You'll keep the candle burning, Brother John?'

'Always, Ieuan, and prayers daily for the poor Prince. He does not deserve this, God knows.'

'The monks at Basingwerk are happy to oblige. Anything

to keep in favour with this spotted King of ours – even excommunicating our Prince.'

The boy had heard of it. The village talked of nothing else, the day it was known: the leaden bell tolling the death of a soul; candles snuffed out, light extinguished; the dreadful chant of the rite of expulsion from God and salvation. Llewelyn, Prince of Wales, was in eternal darkness.

The Abbot was a small, plump man with a smiling face yet I bristled at the sight of him. His eyes were pale blue and watery and the centre was nothing but a prick of black. On the wall behind him was a wooden crucifix, with Our Lord hanging there forever for our sins.

'So this is the physician I've heard of,' he said. My fists curled. 'Well, well, we must make sure you have enough simples to carry you through the autumn.'

And I wondered if it was all in my head, and he was a good man after all.

'You wish to go to the shrine of St Winifrede. How do you know of her, in the Great Fens? You have your own place of pilgrimage.'

'Dafydd – one of the men – he told us the story, Lord Abbot.' I didn't know how to call him. He seemed more lord than holy man. 'He told the story very well.'

'Indeed?' He nodded and smiled and watched us out of his pale blue eyes. 'Well, we must allow you to make your pilgrimage. First, though, you need medicines.'

A silent brother led us through the abbey to the cloister where the herbal was. We had glimpses of new buildings. The refectory was only just finished, the stone still raw but fine in the spare way of the white brothers. We came through to the cloister garden. *Symphytum officinale* was growing there, seeding now, tall and hairy with leaves so prickly they make any part of the body itch; but this has many uses and most of all for wounds and bruises. There was *Ligusticum levisticum* and *Salvia* and *Tanacetum hortis* and many others and Ned had his pick. When he was shown the salves, there was no need to worry, after all. Ned had his own way of doing things. He held them to his nose and sniffed at them and I wanted to laugh and ask who was the half witnow? We packed up the simples and that was the end of it, we thought.

We set off up the valley into the hills to the source of the spring, following the path of the stream. The valley was deep wooded and Squire Phillip and the two men-at-arms were on the alert, listening to every sound. The trees here were alive, shouting gladness through their mossy mouths though their leaves were dull green now, some already bright with autumn. Spiders had spun their webs from the branches and the threads glistened with dewdrops. The stream was glancing from rock to rock, glinting in the sunlight and frothing into eddies. I watched its flow, wondering how it was the water kept moving but the pattern it made falling over the rocks stayed the same. I wanted to spread my hands out like starfish and let the water spill between my fingers and thumbs. Swallows darted ahead of us, swooping and twisting, chasing insects. Soon, they would be gone. We passed the abbey mill, its wheel grinding round, and the lay brothers stopped their work to watch us. The horses clopped up a path that became steeper. Above us was an old castle, not used now, its bank and ditches overgrown already and the keep ruined. Beyond it, in its shelter, was a chapel built long ago, with thick walls, windows and doorway, built in the old style, keeping watch over the well.

We came up to it and looked over the well head into the pool where the water gathered. The well basin was shaped like a star, with five places for folk to sit. Strings of bubbles were rising, like water does when it is heated by fire; but this water was neither hot nor cold, and the brother who kept the chapel told us this was always so, even in the coldest winter. He was an old man. I was thinking I could almost see through his flesh to his backbone, as you see through a threadbare sail to the mast.

'You must lie in the water and pray,' he told us. 'Perhaps this one will regain the power of his tongue.'

'Ned has his own way of speaking,' I said, but I was gentle with the old man. The way he was, and the place itself, made me so. 'He has no need of words.'

He smiled. 'A lucky man, who has no need of words.'

We bathed in the pool and then he filled our containers with the holy water, and gave us his blessing and early apples from a tree that grew near the chapel. We sat down to eat them in sight of the well and the ever-flowing stream. The afternoon sun was warm on our faces and the earth warm beneath us. My body felt light and cool after our bathing and there was clear air to breathe. It seemed that there was no war, only the spirit of peace in this holy place. I was half drowsing, watching Ned take out his knife and cut one of the apples across its middle, so that the seeds showed brown in their star-shaped beds. I wondered what he was thinking, gazing down at it, in a world of his own making. I saw his hand – the one holding the knife – come up to scratch his eyebrow and the point of the knife just missed his eye. He didn't even know. He cut the apple again and fed it to his nag on the palm of his hand. She snuffled it up gustily and nudged him for more.

'Play for us, Ned,' Squire Phillip said quietly, and for a moment I was thinking it was Dick Thatcher who spoke, and I saw then that they were like, but not like; both of them were fair and just and looking out for the next man. I was thinking, then, how it would have been if Dick Thatcher was born the Squire's son. I wished Dick was here with us, not shifting clay on the stinking marsh.

Ned dabbled his hands in the stream and let the water drip from the ends of his fingers. The drops caught the redness of the sun, falling like blood on to the grass. He took out the bone pipe and stroked its smoothness, his mind lingering on some thought of his own. Then he raised the pipe in the way he was taught and I heard the notes the *crwth* had made for the song of St Winifrede. It had not the *crwth's* hundred voices but it was clear and simple for all that, distilled as herbs are to make potions. It came to the part for the *englyn*, and I sang the words under my breath till Squire Phillip said, 'Sing up, Will,' and Sion Sais joined in so we were two voices, one high and one low, singing together with Ned's playing. But we hadn't the words of the story by heart, only the way Dafydd had told it by the camp fire, so that was what we did, jogging our brains, helped on by Ned's playing.

When it was finished, Sion Sais clapped me on the shoulder and said, 'We'll make a Welshman of you yet, boy.' It was then I realised it was Welsh as well as English I'd been using, but it was in Welsh that Dafydd had told the tale, and Sion Sais was speaking to me now in Welsh and it was no use reckoning I didn't understand him. I was red in the face and bothered. Squire Phillip had warned me at Chester that there was danger but now he told us our song was well done and I wanted to think the danger was past but it was the other who worried me, the one who said nothing but stirred the ground with the tip of his knife. I'd seen him sometimes with Bogo, and heard him boast of the men he had killed. The men called him 'the Bull', because he was big and brown and fierce but I was thinking he had wolf's eyes that shone at night like lamps, and a wolf's nature that craved blood. I didn't trust him, though we had shared the day.

Then we came back down the path, the horses stumbling at first over its steepness. We passed the mill, and its turning wheel. We passed by the abbey gates and took the marsh road. The tide had turned and the birds were gathering on mud banks and sand spits. The air was full of their calling. The land opposite seemed very close, as if we could reach out and touch it. Now we could see the high banks and palisades of the camp, and the beginnings of the foundations for the castle walls and, in the landing place we'd made, there was a fleet of rafts and I remembered this was the day they were bringing timber across the river.

We fell silent as we neared the gates. I was thinking that none of us was glad to be back, not even the wolf man whose real name I did not know. And then we were inside and the stench of the place choked us, as it had the day we arrived. Sion Sais swung me down from the horse and steadied me when my legs buckled under me.

'You'd better stick to walking, boy,' he said, but kindly.

We saw Master William coming towards us, passing the tents and makeshift huts and the camp fires. I saw the way the men looked at him, then at us, then away, and there was something in their faces that made me catch my breath. Squire Phillip saw it too. His body was straight and stiff, and he stood with his hand on his nag's halter waiting for Master William to come up to us.

Dick Thatcher was dead.

He'd been helping guide the rafts in. Bogo had been drafted in to help, though he didn't like water. The rafts were heavily loaded with timber and difficult to manage. One of them swung round in the current and caught Bogo off guard. He was swept under the raft. Dick crawled down and hauled him free but the raft grounded with Dick trapped under it and the load of timber tumbled down. They couldn't shift it fast enough. When they did, they found Dick Thatcher dead, face down in the muddy water.

Master William told us.

'*We'll be buried in timber before we're done.*'

'He was old enough to be wed, and had a mind to, but his Mam was dead and there was no girl willing to wed the son because it meant looking after the father as well.'

'Give us a song, Ned,' in that quiet way of his, and the dark mass looming above us.

'Only trees, lads, stag oaks. Nothing to worry about,'

'Not far now, Will, not far now.'

Let's build up the fire again. I'm cold, cold, remembering. So many years ago but it chills me now to think of that glad day we had up in the hills and Dick Thatcher choking in Dee mud just when he was in my mind and I was wishing him with us.

We sang of the miracle of St Winifrede while that good man was dying. No breathing life into his head, though the good God knows his father tried. Not all the waters of the well could bring him back. And John Thatcher, whose tongue was sharp as the tip of a spear, sobbed like a woman and would not be comforted. He held his dead son in his arms like Mary with the dead Christ, but he was the one pierced and tormented. We hadn't understood: he loved his son.

Peter Long said, 'We got him to let go and lie down. We thought maybe we could get him to sleep but he caught sight of Bogo and he was up and yelling. It frightened shit out of me, I can tell you.'

'What did he do?'

'Got hold of a knife and tried to kill Bogo. The Northman got it off him – he's a slash down his arm needs looking at, Ned.'

'Bogo?'

'Safe. He must have a charmed life. He didn't lift a finger. Won't hear a word against John. Says if he'd had a son like Dick, he'd have done the same.' Peter stopped and his voice shook. 'Wouldn't we all?' His Adam's apple worked up and down as if he was Walter Reed.

'Where's John now?' Squire Phillip asked.

'Lying down like a dead man. He won't answer.'

We went with them, Ned and me, to where Dick Thatcher was laid out on a stretch of the timber that had killed him. They'd washed him, and his face was calm, like it always was, though his eyes were fast shut.

John Thatcher was inside our shelter, curled up, his face to the wall. He didn't speak or move, not even when he felt Ned's hand on his head, but he let us turn him on to his back and let Ned lift him and spoon him sips of water from the holy well. Ned sat with him all night long, and Bogo kept watch outside, keeping the fire burning. A fire is a fine thing for comfort. Ned played on the swan pipe all the night through; songs to quiet the soul and bring peace to the mind and help for the heart. I didn't know. I was asleep, tired out with the day and with grief.

† I've thought much about it since. How we think we know each other but this is not true. We are the same but not the same. Nothing is constant except the illimitable, everlasting music of the firmament. Everything else is subject to change, and we poor humans are the most changeable. Maybe – just maybe – the human soul has in its depths the constancy of the firmament. Maybe it can resonate to the same sounds. I have been thinking of this lately. If so, there is hope for us mortals in this sorry world.

My son, child of my hearth,
My one son,
I weep for your loss.

Cold and bitter my tears,
brine like the sea,
the treacherous sea.
You sleep cold tonight.
I cannot sleep
for the clangour of grief
that afflicts me.
I shall sing songs in your praise.
Man of peace,
Man of honour,
Man of courage in danger,
Man strong and steadfast.
You covered me with warmth
like a thick cloak.
You spread before me a table
of good things.
Oh my son, child of my hearth,
My one son,
I weep for you.

He was the first I mourned with words. Ned helped me set my song to music and I sang it for John Thatcher. I borrowed from the old songs, as you no doubt noted – well, I was young then and not yet learning my craft. The old songs carry comfort even now, in spite of all these new fashions.

September passed into October and the high tides came. More fossatores were sent to Rhuddlan but we stayed, digging ditches for the King. I kept thinking of one of the

Welshman's songs: an old song, from time past.

There is a fine fortress
stands in the sea.
Ask, oh Britain, who rightly
owns it.

The camp was a prison and we were without hope. Every day brought hardship. At the end of September, Squire Phillip left, along with his men-at arms and his bony hounds and sagging nag. His time of fealty was done, and we should have gone with him, but times were changing, and we were Edward's men now, his fossatores, his ditch diggers who made land out of water. He wouldn't let us go. Squire Phillip didn't like it but what could he do? It was the King's order. At least Squire Phillip was given leave to take Walter with him and we were glad for the old man and his skinny wife. Walter's eyes were moist when he left us and his throat wobbled. I didn't want to laugh at him now, and when he stroked my hair and kissed me I was shamed to tears.

One dark night, John Thatcher walked out into the high tide and shifting sands. Ned and me, we saw him go but did not stop him. We never found his body.

Six

Stand here, at the meeting point of these four roads. See how their ways converge on this place. One road winds through woodland; the second rises and falls over hills and valleys; the third quivers across marshland; the fourth follows the plough across the folds of fields. Yet all four arrive here. And so it is with the four disciplines of the quadrivium: arithmetic, geometry, astronomy and music. All follow their own paths, searching for truth. Yet out of these four it is music alone that concerns itself with morality: it is music that affects all humanity. Whether young or aged, no one is excluded from the charm of sweet song.

All Hallows. White fog blinding the marshes. It smothered the river. It twisted over the camp like a wraith come early to All Souls. We shivered in the dank morning and our bodies ached with cold. At least we had hot food to warm our bellies.

'They say the Leopard's starving Llewelyn into surrender,' Peter Long said. 'Now he has Anglesey grain, there's nothing left for Llewelyn and his wretches but bare rock to gnaw on, poor devils.'

'Keep your voice down, man. Ears everywhere, these days.'

'They say the King gave orders to ruin the harvest,' Thomas Wytheberd said.

'Don't be a halfwit. Of course he didn't – he's feeding his own men with it. Crafty, is Edward.'

'Maybe if Llewelyn gives himself up, we can be home by Christmas.' Gil Allbone was thinner, sadder, pining for his plump wife. He was more muddled in his mind than ever since Dick and John Thatcher were dead and I wished Squire Phillip had taken him home as well as Walter.

Peter Long cackled. 'You think the Leopard will let us go now? The masons and carpenters will down tools for the winter but us ditchers are going to dig our way to hell before he says stop.'

'If hell is hot with fire, as the good fathers say, I would welcome it,' the Northman said and puffed out his cheeks so that his breath added more mist to the white air. I huddled next to him, warming my hands on a bowl of porridge and listening to the talk.

'Edward's back in Shrewsbury,' someone said. 'He must think it's safe to leave Wales.'

I said, 'Edward's coming here tomorrow.'

'Been listening at tent flaps again, young Will?' said Peter Long. I nodded. Now I was the one to know the latest news, not Peter Long, and they listened to me as if I was a grown man, not a stripling.

'On his way from Shrewsbury,' I said.

'Stopping here?'

'No. Going on to Rhuddlan.'

'Wonder if he'll take any of us with him this time?'

He did. He arrived on All Souls, so we could not pray for Dick and John or leave food for them. It was the first time I could remember that we had not kept the two sacred days. Not Edward. He spent the night at Basingwerk and left on the third day; he took Peter Long and the Northman and Gil Allbone. So out of the eight from our village that left just Ned and me. Harold Edmundson didn't like it. He told Richard the Engineer it wasn't right to leave us two behind but he might as well have stayed silent. It only got him black marks and black looks and the threat of worse. I thanked him for trying. He was grim faced.

'This I do not like, young Will. You must take care. You and Ned, you are being watched.'

'I don't know what you mean.' But I did.

'It's true, Will,' said Peter Long. 'The Bull shadows you. I've watched him. Ears and eyes, Will, everywhere these days.'

I shivered. I was thinking of wolf's eyes shining at night like lamps, and the wolf's nature that craved blood. I was thinking as well about the Welshman and if they knew about him being at the abbey last winter after all. A man who made trouble, Ralf said, and used his music to turn folk against the King, working on them like a smith: earth, water, fire, air. But it wasn't true. His music made harmony. Our Abbot himself had given welcome to Ieuan ap y Gof. I had heard their talk. It was the King who struck false notes; he was the leopard that feasted on living flesh, but to say so was to ask for death.

'Who can Llewelyn trust?'

'You, and men like you.'

'Take care, Will.'

'Look out for Ned.'

'I've been looking out for Ned for as long as I know.' Did I say that? Was it my voice that sounded so tired? So bitter?

'This is so, Will. You have done well. You are a good boy – a good brother, a good son and a good friend. Soon, all this will end. You will see.' The Northman nodded.

Gil Allbone said nothing. He put his arms round Ned, then me, and gave us the kiss of kinship, and I hugged him back and wondered if I would ever see him again.

'Stick with it, young 'un,' said Peter Long. 'We'll soon be home.' For a moment I was thinking about the girl on the wharf and the baby in her belly and I wondered if Peter Long was thinking of her as well. A wife and a child and a home and hearth. It seemed good to me.

† Of course, he's long dead now, Peter. He died in the winter of '93, from the ague. He came back from the wars and would have married the wench, but she hadn't waited. She'd married as soon as she could, to give the bastard a name. Peter went north for a time with Godfrey Northumberland, then, one summer's day, he turned up in the village with a northern lass and a couple of bairns and set up home with no more of his wild ways. I wasn't there. I was wandering the world by then, telling my stories to whoever would listen. His grandson is the spit of him in more than looks. I heard tell there's a small matter of stolen eels to be settled, too. Well, well – same but not the same, wouldn't you say? As for Gil Allbone, he came home but he was mazed. His plump wife took him in

and cared for him but he was broken. He swore in God's name that he saw the marsh lights and one night he followed them. Walter Reed saved him that time but he set out again, another night. He was found face down in a pool. They said he looked peaceful in death.

We watched them, that raw November morning, marching out of the town gate behind Edward's soldiers. We watched from the palisade long after they were swallowed into the whiteness and I was thinking again about the day we watched the Welshman and Gwydion until they vanished into the air – and I knew then how Ned had felt, and how dogs feel when they howl their grief. My heart was heavy with misery. I was alone, and looking out for Ned was too hard for me with the Bull breathing on our backs. I barely spoke to a soul, all that day – not that there was much of a day. Hardly was it noon before chill night set in, shivering our bones and bodies. We were as gloomy as the day, sitting by our smouldering fire.

The third day of November was St Winifrede's. That was one and two and three, all holy days. All day long, Ned was churning things in his mind. At dusk, when he gurgled his plans, I was worried.

'Ned, the holy well? Tonight? No; that's daft.'

I knew it was useless. Once Ned made up his mind, nothing stopped him. He needed more holy water and tonight it would be twice blessed. No hope now of asking leave to go, not from William of March, not from Richard the Engineer. I wondered what they'd do to us, if we were found out, and if there was any tale to tell to keep us safe. I shivered. Then I was thinking about the valley and the woods and the hidden mouths behind their mossy covering and the white mist coiling itself around the marshland, and the old castle crumbling back into the earth and the ghosts that flitted about after All Souls and I was afraid.

Ned wasn't. He slipped out into the night, his beaky nose snuffing out the way.

Behind the mist the sky seemed lit up by the moon, though it was but half full. It seemed we were alone in a lost world, like they say the dead are when they lie between this one and the next. We stopped to listen. The air was filled with the soft whistles of night fowl, and the damp, mouldy stench of the riverbank. White mist drifted and spread and scattered and I saw river mud glisten under the stars. I was thinking about the marsh dragons and the beasts that dragged you under and I was afraid. I felt the taste of the marsh mud in my mouth, and remembered how wet clay clogged my ears and my nostrils. I thought how the ugly things under the mud would come and get me. But Ned was there, and Ned would keep me safe.

Marsh grass slithered under our feet. The greedy slap and suck of the outgoing tide dragged at the riverbanks and I wished there was a strong sea wall between us and the swirling river, like we had at home. I wished then that we were at home, even if it was with Mam's heavy hand raised against me, and all this fear and dirt and cold but a dream.

The sleeping camp was swallowed up in mist. I could smell fire smoke and hear low mutters from the men on night watch, then Bogo's throaty laugh and louder laughter from the men and I knew it was woman talk. The Bull was with them. I had looked for him when we crept by, remembering the Northman's warning words, and he was there, knife out, whittling at a staff. I saw how firelight flashed on cold metal and heard the rasp of the blade.

We had to make it there and back before dawn. Ned knew the way. Of course he did. He always knew the way. He set out across the marsh as if he were walking the fen track back home.

Ahead of him, the attenuated shape was hunched black against the bright moon. It seemed to glide along the track, sure-footed and unafraid of the deep, still pools where the marsh devils lurked. The boy struggled to keep up on stubby little legs but sobs choked his throat and he was afraid of being left behind. Wait for me! His voice couldn't carry across the great, flat expanse of marshland. It was a gasp of air, breathless and piping like a curlew's call.

Ned halted at the edge of the marsh where the hills stepped off into the whiteness. Water dripped through branches that were now mostly bare of leaves. Somewhere on the edge of hearing there was skittering and rustling. An owl swooped low and we both jerked back, startled. I was shivering with fright. Now, I didn't want to leave the muddy smell of the marsh. Not our fen marsh, true, but safe for all that. Same but not the same. My teeth set up achatter and Ned swivelled his head towards me. His face was wraith pale and his eyes were glowing. He grinned and his hand came up to push back his thatch of hair and I was thinking about all the other times we'd been out in the night and come home safe. I thought of the holy lady. This was her day and her night and we were about her work. If it was her will, she'd keep us safe enough. I tried to grin back, though it was more like grinding my teeth, but Ned knew what I meant. He always did.

We set off up the track we'd followed on horseback on a day when summer stayed late and we didn't know Dick Thatcher would be dead before night. We kept the dripping trees on our left and the rushing water on our right. The sound was deafening. Now and again we saw white foam and then we knew we were too close to the river. I was thinking about how easy a way it had been, high on the back of a nag, with no need to watch where I was putting my feet. Now I was slithering about in wet grass and churned mud and fearful of slipping into the black water. I couldn't help thinking then of Dick Thatcher trapped under the heap of timber, his mouth and nose full of mud and slime. I wondered how he had faced his death and if he'd felt fear. Perhaps he did, even Dick Thatcher, who had nothing to fear in the next life.

Once I looked back and thought I saw wolf's eyes shining like lamps, and a shadow shape lurking where the track twisted, but it might just as well have been a swirl of mist.

The wall of the chapel loomed white in front of our noses. We could see the dim light of the candle flickering inside but this time there was no Brother to greet us. I wished he had been there to give us his blessing and a gift of apples like small moons from the tree that grew near the chapel. Then I was thinking of Ralf and taking apples from the Abbey trees and how the wetness dripped from the leaves of the trees, smacking from leaf to leaf and splashing cold on my forehead, as it did now when I stared up through the bare branches.

Ned nudged me and we crept to the well head; we filled the flasks we had brought with us and strapped them again to our belts. They were hard and knobbly against my body. I was glad Ned was there. It made it all right with God and holy Winifrede, if Ned was there. All the same, I muttered a prayer and gave thanks for the holy water.

The wind was rising and the mist shifted long enough to let the moon light up the well. A gleam shot across the dark water and lit up Ned's hunched-heron shape. He was still as a stone, listening. Even his bones held stillness.

Motionless, like a heron, with sunlight striking off him. It glinted through stained glass windows in a prism of light: red, blue, green, gold, flickering on walls and altar. And on Ned. It lit on his cheeks, the end of his nose, his forehead. The boy halted in the church door and gazed and gazed at his brother, kneeling before the altar, radiant in light. Somewhere, a voice was calling but he took no heed. Nothing mattered except this moment. This was his brother, the all wise, the hunched heron. 'Look out for him', said Mam, and the boy knew that was his destiny. *Look out for him.*

I heard an owl's ghost call, and another, and a noise that was not an owl at all but it was too late. I was gripped by hard hands that choked the cry out of me and shoved me hard down with my head over the edge of the water. My arms were wrenched round behind my back, almost ripped out of their arm joints, so that the pain of it tore through my body. There was no sound. I was thinking maybe it was God's anger that had come down on us but the stench of sour breath was real enough. The Bull? Fear forced sick up into my throat. I gagged and tried to spit but a rough hand was clamped over my mouth and a heavy knee ground into the small of my back, forcing me down.

'Easy with him – he's nothing but a young lad.'

'Even the young have teeth and claws.'

Low mutters but I caught the Welsh. Not the Bull, then. The hand eased and I squirmed and bit down into the fleshy part of the thumb. The man swallowed his yelp of pain.

'And this one has more than his share of teeth. He's taken a piece out of me!"

'Met your match, Bryn?'

'Now don't, for Our Lady's sake, be telling me to go gentle with the skinny brute. What's a boy doing here, anyway, this time of night?'

'That's for us to find out. Hood him and let's get them both away from here. If it's a trap, we don't want to spring it.'

'Not a whisper out of you, boy.' A blade flashed close to my face. My eyes must have been as big as the moon at the full. He nodded and heaved me to my feet. I tried to look round for Ned but something rough and coarse was pulled over my head and shoulders and down over my body so I was trussed like one of the Squire's geese ready for the pot. I could barely breathe, much less see. I was hoisted over the man's shoulder. He wasn't much taller than me and he grunted with my weight and shifted me. More ease for him, I was thinking, but not for me, with my head banging against his back when he set off striding away from the water. Not much taller but strong. The sound of water grew distant. Over it came the chink of bridle and the soft snort of a nag cut off short. Stifled, most like.

'What have you got there?' The voice was quiet, deadened so as not to carry.

'Two Sais rats thieving water from the holy well.' It was the one called Bryn who spoke. I was dumped on the ground and the cloth pulled away from my face. I gasped in the cold air. I could hear Ned next to me, breathing hard. I wished I could see him. I hoped they hadn't hurt him.

'They're from the camp. We watched them come up.'

'Only these two?'

'That's all – this one's a stripling. With teeth, mind you. The other's a lanky sort, no meat on him. Didn't put up any sort of a fight.'

'They've courage enough, coming up here on a night like this – not likely they've permission to be outside the camp, either. Sure they were alone?'

'We kept a good lookout, Islwyn.'

The third voice – Islwyn's – was impatient. 'Let's hope you did. The last thing we want is Edward's men on our backs. Hoist these two aboard. We've finished here.'

I was gulping like a landed fish, trying to find my voice; the Welsh words that would tell them we were friends, not foe, but it was too late. The same rough hands grabbed me and slung me over the nag. The man swung himself up into the saddle. I had no more than a glimpse of three shapes of men. I tried to rake my wits together but they'd scattered wide. I didn't know what was worse: to be caught by the Bull or by Llewelyn's men. And was there any tale that would get us out of this mire? The men urged their nags to a sharp trot in spite of the night. I tried to catch my breath in time to the rise and fall, thankful they'd left the cloth open wide enough for mouthfuls of air. Sodden ground and leaf fall muffled the horses' hooves. I opened my eyes once only and shut them tight when I saw the ground spinning by and branches stretching out claws. I was thinking that falling into the everlasting pit of hellfire could not be worse than this jolting ride through the night.

The nags strained uphill. Their breath came steaming into the misty night and was swallowed by it. At last we clopped over stones into a yard. A shape moved forward out of the shadows and reached for the bridle.

'We've brought company, Twm.' It was Islwyn who spoke.

'Company's welcome, as long as you've brought no trouble with it. Not followed?'

'No – but stay on watch, all the same. All well here?'

'All's well.'

I was pulled down off the nag and the sacking torn from my head. The night air was cold and fresh and I gulped it in. I was dizzy and shaking from the journeying. I tottered on my feet, glad now of the heavy sacking against the chill night. Ahead of us was the dark mass of a building. The mist was clearing and the moon shone on wasted walls and blind windows. An old hall; long forsaken.

'Move – come on, brat.' The man called Bryn thumped me onwards. I stumbled and he jerked me upright and kept a clutch on my shoulder, dragging and pushing me through a doorway. The door was reeling back against its frame. An oak door bound with iron. A fine door in its time. The draughty passage was black as a raven's wing and stank of scorched wood and burned thatch. We turned through another archway and into the hall.

It was dark. The window openings were shuttered but there was a fire burning on the hearth in the middle of the room and there was a burnt stench, too, that was not living fire at all. It was warm after the cold night. The flames and smoke flickered up to darkness. Part of the roof gaped open to the night sky and stars spilled through. In the light of the fire I could see the shapes of men. One of them stepped forward.

'So, Islwyn, you've brought guests.' His voice was deep and quiet.

'Yes, my lord. Bryn and Elfyn invited them.'

My lord? This man was dressed in rough brown cloth, like any of us workmen. He was short and stocky with dark hair and dark eyes. His eyebrows were thick like seeding grass. He was clean shaven but with a long moustache. I had seen men like him in the camp at Chester, but this one was not the same. I looked again. He stood like a leader, and the man Islwyn bowed to him, yet his face was quiet, like his voice, and I felt a flicker of hope. This man was not a fierce beast ready to spring and kill with one leap.

'Did they indeed? I hope our guests came willingly?'

'That I cannot say, my lord. I was not there when they were asked.'

'So? And where were you?' The brows shot up each time he said, 'So.'

'Tending the horses, my lord, and keeping lookout.'

He nodded. 'Let me see these guests of ours. Take off their wrappings. It's warm enough in here. You must have been afraid they would catch cold.' A shaft of laughter lit his voice. 'We entertain young boys these days. What is your name, child?'

The man called Islwyn said, 'They are Sais, my lord Ithel.'

'So?' He asked again, in careful Norman, 'What is your name, child?'

'Wilfred,' I said, 'and this is my brother Edmund.' I spoke in Welsh and stared him in the face. 'We were not invited, Lord Ithel. We were taken by force from the holy well.'

'So? A Sais boy who speaks our tongue.' His brows shot up again and his eyes were alert, like a kestrel that stoops. I was thinking I would die rather than let him see me shake.

'Yes, my lord, and two who mean you no harm.'

I stared him in the face and gritted my teeth when laughter crossed his face again. Then he was grave.

'What were you doing at the holy well tonight?'

No slow speech now; this was arrow shot.

'We came to ask the holy Winifrede for help and for her blessing. We need water from the well for our sick.'

'But you come by night like thieves.'

I was stung. 'We are not thieves.'

'Has your Richard the Engineer sent you?'

I was thinking how we had sneaked out and blushed. 'No, my lord.'

'No? You come by yourselves, then?'

'Yes, my lord.'

'So? You can come and go as you please? Two boys?'

I tilted my head up. 'We did not ask leave. We came of our own will to ask the help of the lady Winifrede.'

'And you think our Welsh lady will help Edward's cause?'

'I pray she will help all who are suffering, my lord.' I stopped. I was thinking hard. 'There are many of us who were not invited to go to war, my lord,' I said. My voice was as dry as if I'd been John Thatcher.

'So?' His eyebrows shot up. He stared back. 'You are a bold boy. What about your friend here? Why doesn't he speak?'

'He is my brother and he cannot speak, my lord. At least, he does but not many understand him.'

'An idiot?'

'No!'

'So. A lion cub defending its own.' The shaft of laughter was back in his voice but I was bristling. The man watched me and his face grew sad. 'It's a good thing to see, boy, and it were better for us all if brother did not turn against brother.' I knew as if he spoke the words aloud that he was thinking of Llewelyn and his brother Dafydd, who was his sworn foe, and another brother kept captive in a castle prison. I turned to my own brother. Ned was smiling, smiling as if he were among friends. I looked to where he was gazing and then I knew.

A man was sitting in the deep shadow of the wall. He held a *crwth* and had, maybe, been tuning it before we came in. Maybe playing. It wasn't Ieuan. Ned's eyes held fast on the *crwth*.

'So.' I was starting to wait for the word. 'Your brother watches our bard. Perhaps he would like to take a turn?'

Ned twisted towards him and was nodding and smiling and gurgling. I said, 'Yes.'

'So…' This time he dragged out the word. 'He can play?'

'Yes.'

'So.' He stopped. He was thinking. He spoke over my head to the *crwth* player. 'Llygad, as a favour to me, lend this guest your *crwth*. He will play for us since you cannot.'

Ned was bowing and smiling at the player. His head nodded up and down like a jackdaw.

'You think he can be no worse than me, my lord?' said the man Llygad. I saw then that he held his bow hand carefully against his side; his hand was wrapped in linen and blood had soaked through and dried in a black crust. Ned touched the hand lightly, peering at the cloth as if he was trying to see through it to the wounds beneath. The man sighed and held out the *crwth* with his good hand.

'Why not? Let's see how a Sais plays – if he can play. I just hope he doesn't snap the strings. I've none to spare.'

Ned took the *crwth* in both hands and stroked its wooden side and the bridge. He shivered the strings and frowned and sat down on a stool with the *crwth* on his knee and started to tighten the tuning pins.

The men laughed and joked. A Sais who knew how to tune a *crwth*? A Sais who couldn't even speak? I said nothing. I knew what would happen. Llygad said nothing, either, but watched the way Ned cradled the *crwth*. Ned's head was bent, listening. He plucked one of the strings then another and nodded again and ran his fingers over all six strings. Four over the bridge and two in free air. He lifted the crwth and passed its leather strap about his neck. He held the *crwth* sideways to his body, as he had been taught. He was not smiling and nodding now but grave and intent and the men stopped their joking and watched him in silence.

'Take your time, boy,' the music master said. 'Position the *crwth* so that it is part of you, another limb. Feel it

– it is alive. Feel it quiver under your bow and vibrate through your body. Feel it, boy?'

The lanky, hunched figure nodded. His face was ecstatic. The hand gripping the curved bow was shaking.

'Gently, boy, gently. You're holding that bow as if you're going to stab meat. Wait. Put it down. First, empty your mind. Get rid of the swaddling cloth that's stifling you. Let your arms hang like dead eels. Breathe. Yes, boy, now take up the bow. Let the *crwth* breathe with you. Let it be part of you. But remember that you, the *crwth*, the bow are nothing more than a vessel; an empty vessel waiting to be filled with music.'

Winter sunshine poured through the abbey window, glancing off red hair, black hair: two faces remote, serious, their souls away and separate from the husks of their bodies.

Slowly now, the black-haired boy raised his arm, curving over the instrument. He swept the bow across the strings and the first notes straddled the silence.

I shall always remember that time, that place, that night of mist and danger and Ned holding the *crwth* and the bow as if nothing else in the world mattered. And it didn't, for him – nor, perhaps, for us. Those first notes. Oh, they shivered through the hall and the men stopped all laughter. The hair on our heads stood on end. The bow swept across the strings and the *crwth* sobbed and cried. Under the top notes a low lamenting went on and on. It was as if we had died and our souls were born again.

He played Ieuan ap y Gof's song, the first song we had heard the music man play. It was the song Ned had played on the swan-bone pipe the day he watched Ieuan dwindle out of his life along the fen path. It was the song he had played on the ramparts in Chester and that had landed us in trouble with the Welsh Marcher lord. Now he played it again on a borrowed *crwth* in an ancient, half-ruined hall. The hot flames of the fire leapt up to meet the cold light of stars dropping through the empty spaces in the roof and I swear for an instant we heard their music.

'Well Father Abbot, we have an audience of two mice.'

I watched them, the four Welshmen, making a still circle around the hub of Ned's playing. Outside was the fifth man, the one they called Twm, keeping watch in the chill night for foes at the door.

And suddenly there was a sixth listener. A woman came into the room in a little rush. She was holding a bairn to her.

'Ieuan?' she called and her voice broke joyfully across the music. Ned stopped and the music stopped with him. 'Ieuan?' she said again, but uncertain this time. She looked around the room, her eyes wide with wonder when they lighted on Ned. 'I thought it was Ieuan come to find us,' she said.

She was beautiful. Every storyteller knows that. We all know how to describe how her hair is loose about her shoulders and black as the raven or gold as the risen sun or her lips like a thread of scarlet. It is our trade. We weave dreams about our beautiful maiden, fair as the moon, clear as the sun. I have learned the art. All over the world, listeners want to know how she was beautiful. They lean towards me, their faces lit, eyes bright, lips moist. Her mouth? Her eyes? Her body? And I tell them in rolling phrases and cadences what they yearn to know.

This woman? How could I say? I was only a boy but I remember her as beautiful with a beauty that comes from the soul. Her hair was, I think, brown – maybe fair – and braided. Her gown was as homespun as the men's and hanging loose on her slight frame. The bairn she held to her was no more than a twelve month and swaddled in thick woollens. The firelight played over them both. Maybe it was her eyes, as clear as the windows in the Brothers' great abbey church, clear and luminous; the eyes of doves by the rivers of waters.

'It was Ieuan's song…'

'We have two guests, Angharad; Wilfred and Edmund.' He glanced a warning but Ned's ears had already pricked and his eyes were fixed on the lady's shining face. He made a clumsy little bow and played again. I knew the starting notes; this time a sweet song that praised a maid's beauty. And he sang. The sound poured out as sweet as ever Gwydion sang for Ieuan ap y Gof. I gaped, my mouth dropping open. I had never heard him sing before – never heard more than gurgled words. This was the first time. There was only ever one time more.

'This song is for my lord's lady,' the music man said. 'She is Angharad, a lady of great beauty and goodness.' He turned to the golden youth standing by his side. 'Gwydion; this time don't forget the rising note in the sixth line. You missed it when we practised yesterday.'

Gwydion scowled but even then, to the watching boy, he was beautiful, standing tall and slight under the graceful curves of the stone arch, waiting for the sign to begin the song.

Through the clear glass of the window the sky was the cold, bright blue of fine winter days. A skein of geese arrowed past, necks stretched and wings creaking. On the tree outside the window a plump robin flitted from one bare branch to another and a blackbird hunched its shoulders against the sharp wind. In the split second before the music man struck the first note, the blackbird – no doubt thinking it was spring come already – opened his throat and sang. The boy heard its piercing sweet call and then the murmur of voices as Brother John and Brother Peter passed by.

A ray of light struck through the window. It glanced off the arch and across Gwydion's face and spilled on to the tiled floor. It fastened on the threads of horsehair in the music man's bow and they glistened as if they were precious metal. It lit up the six strings of the *crwth* and it seemed to the boy that even the notes shimmered as they fell through the air.

Ned sang one verse then stopped. For a blink of time I was thinking he would speak. He didn't. He stood still with the bow dangling from one hand and the *crwth* strapped around his neck and the firelight glinting on him.

'But how is this?' said the Lady Angharad. 'You play Ieuan's songs. You sing my own song, the one that Ieuan made for me alone.'

And then, of course, I had to tell the tale and it sounded odd in my own ears: an English village boy learning the craft of a Welsh bard? Taught by a *pencerdd* himself? How likely was that? And then the boy couldn't even talk like others talked. How could they know he was clever? But I should have known. Ned had already told the tale. He had played like the angels themselves. Like the stars singing, if we could only hear them.

We were given food to eat and wine, the first time I had tasted it. This was what the Normans had, then, this drink that was red like day-old blood. I liked ale better. The food was rough, not as good as we had in the camp. There were oatcakes and cheese with a hard rind and strips of dried meat.

'Blame your King,' said Bryn. 'He's starving us out.'

'Cymer – that's where we are going. Ieuan was hurt in the Dolforwyn siege but we heard he escaped west to where he knew there were men loyal to Llewelyn. The white brothers are taking care of him. They will give him back his health. It is an abbey that is loyal to our Prince.'

Islwyn the careful said, 'They have hidden him. No one knows he is alive, let alone at the abbey.'

'But you tell us?'

'You are his friends.'

Two mice.

'Where is Cymer?'

'South west from here. We shall follow in Gwenfrewi's footsteps – Winifrede, you would say. In her second life, she journeyed from Holywell to Bodfari and from there to the old place of the saints, Henllan, and from there to Gwytherin, to the nunnery where she lived out her second life and died and was buried there. Until the monks of Shrewsbury came for her sacred bones and took them to England. All our sacred relics go to England. At least Llewelyn has the Croes Nawdd safe with him. And may it save our Prince from the outcast places.'

It was fitting that this splinter of the True Cross, this most holy relic that the Welsh called the Cross of Refuge, was carried by one scorned and cast out. Don't you agree? Maybe not. Don't answer. He was wearing it, you know, when he was ambushed and killed that terrible day, and his head cut from his body. Edward took the holy relic. He robbed Wales of its great treasure. He did the same for Scotland, years later. A cunning man, Edward. Spotted, like the leopard.

'After that it's south, following the old straight road, down to God's place on earth.' Bryn grinned with pleasure, short arms hugging his stocky, short body.

My Lord Ithel laughed. He was at ease now, no longer raising his eyebrows like weapons. 'Bryn speaks of the Mawddach. It is his bro – his land. He loves it above all other places. And why not? All Welshmen love the place of their birth.'

'And you, my lord, in your turn, love your bro,' said Bryn. 'And that, young Will, is why we defend ourselves against your Edward. This land is ours.'

'Not 'my' Edward,' I said. 'He never was our King, in the Great Fens. Men have long memories, there. We remember what he did.'

Later, they spoke of Ieuan.

'He was our *bardd teulu* – our own musician, belonging to our family. You do not have such a thing in England. And now he is a *pencerdd*, a great musician, and known through all Wales. More than this, he is our good friend. He needs our help. It's only a matter of time, now, before Llewelyn surrenders,' said Lord Ithel. 'Edward is too strong and he is a clever leader, whatever else he may be. He's made sure his army is supplied by sea. Now, he rules all ways to Wales. Anglesey is cut off and with it the food that should supply our men. Llewelyn is trapped in Snowdon and the weather is closing in. Llewelyn won't let his men starve. He'll surrender.'

'And we are building the castles that will rule Wales,' I said.

'It's not your fault. You had no choice.'

I was thinking about leaving our land and the long journey across England and the three men-at-arms herding us to Chester.

'No,' I said. 'We had no choice.'

Ned was grinning and smiling. Ieuan ap y Gof was alive. I was thinking about the day we left Boston and how I had laughed at the thought that we would find Ned's Welshman, one man amongst so many.

'You should come with us,' said Bryn. He grinned. 'Those sharp teeth of yours would do better than any guard dog's.'

I glowered at him and his grin grew wider.

Angharad said, 'For shame, Bryn, don't tease the boy.'

'Why not? He's had a strip of my hide – I'll have a piece of his.' He slapped my shoulder with a strength that almost sat me on my backside. I pummelled his broad chest. He held me off, laughing loudly. 'Peace, boy, peace! Call him off, Master Ned!'

Everybody was laughing now and me with them. Bryn ruffled my hair. 'I mean what I say: come with us.'

'Yes, come with us,' said Angharad. Her eyes shone as if candles were lit behind them. 'Why go back to that terrible place?'

They knew, now, the story of our coming to Flint.

'But they'll hunt for us.'

'And you'll be far away. Come with us. You are our family now.'

Ned pulled at my sleeve. Ieuan ap y Gof. That was all he thought of. To be with Ieuan again, his *pencerdd*, his music master. I was thinking about the brown, dull prison of the camp and the endless footings for the castle and the stench of living there. I was thinking about Dick drowned under timbers; Peter Long and Godfrey Northumberland crushed into a cage waiting for judgement because they had killed a sheep. I was thinking about the Bull and how he watched us. Winter was coming and they would keep us working long after the carpenters and masons had finished for the season. And for what? To crush Wales and Llewelyn, its last prince. And all at Edward's word, the Leopard, the King who was ruthless and cruel and who cared nothing for the little men, the workers.

Ned pulled at my sleeve again. I was opening my mouth to say yes, we would go with them. And then it was that the old door to the hall burst open and the Bull was there, with armed men at his back.

They took us by surprise. No word of alarm from Twm, no cry or shout of warning.

What could we do to defend ourselves?

Elfyn was slain on a sword thrust. He died with his eyes

wide open and his hand fumbling at his sword belt. Islwyn's throat was slashed before he could speak. His choking sounded in my ears and I saw the spurt of blood that was his life spilling out on to the floor of the hall. Bryn's arms were wrenched back and gripped by two burly soldiers, both a head taller, while a third ripped him open from stem to stern. My Lord Ithel stood his ground. He held his broad sword high. And the Bull and his men closed in.

The woman ran in front of their swords. Her braids swung out around her and the child was howling in her arms. The world slowed to a dead stop. The Bull swung his sword. It curved in a great, sweeping arc and its shining edge hacked into the place where her shoulder joined her neck. There was a dreadful sound of iron on flesh. She dropped like a stone and her eyes, her bright, clear eyes, flashed towards heaven. The child dropped from her arms. Lord Ithel cried out as she fell. The Bull shifted his grip and grabbed the sword by its blade and smashed the hilt down on my lord's skull and split it, crushing it like an egg, and Lord Ithel was slaughtered. The Bull laughed and swung again and the child was spitted on his steaming sword.

I was gaping with horror, gasping for breath. I saw my lady fall dead, and my lord, and the child, and blood flowing red like the wine we had drunk, and all the peace and harmony that was between us shattered. Ned was in my sight, his hands reaching for my lady. The Bull lifted his sword again. Then Bogo was bellowing at me, 'Go, boy, go,' and I saw him running at the Bull, his short sword lifted ready to plunge. I didn't know what he meant at first. He cried again, 'Go! Run!' and I knew then he was giving us the chance to escape. Bogo the bellower who had snorted and sneered at us, Bogo the pillock, was giving us the chance of life. True, he owed us life thrice over: Dick had saved him from the muddy waters of the Dee, Ned had salved his wound and the Northman had saved him from John Thatcher, but this was not the same. We should have been slaughtered, there in the old hall, together with the King's foes but Bogo had chosen to give us life. It's not easy choosing. I like to think he had chosen to let the saint in but that thought came much later. Then, I gaped and gasped at the blood that gushed in front of my eyes.

'Run!'

I grabbed at Ned and we stumbled towards the door. At the edge of my sight I saw Bogo flailing at the Bull but it was going hard against him and I knew he would fail. We were out in the night air, in the yard. Stretched across the cobbles, as if he were asleep, was Twm. I knew he was dead. The nags were snorting and stamping, frighted by the noise and bloodshed. I started towards them and stopped. What to do? Ned was mazed. His mouth was wide open and his eyes wider. He was shaking and I suppose I was as well. I dragged him to the stalls, thinking to escape on one of the nags but the nearest one pulled away from me, rearing up, and I knew it was hopeless. I stopped. I was thinking, thinking harder and faster than ever in my life.

I hustled Ned out of the stable and into the deep shadows of the trees. I held a finger to my mouth. 'Not a sound,' I hissed. 'Stay here. Wait for me.' I went back to the horses and dragged at their halters. My hands were shaking badly and my fingers fumbled on the loops as I tried to loose them. Then they slackened and the nags were free. I kept clear of their back legs and their metal-shod hooves, flapped my hands and hushed at them until they leaped away in a rush into the dark, their hooves striking sparks from the stones.

I shrank next to Ned, pulling us both into the safe shadow of the trees. I never gave a thought to their gnarled staring faces and shouting mouths. I only counted them as friends who would shelter us as they sheltered all hunted creatures.

The Bull burst out, and the men after him. I could hear their breathing heavy like animals as they clustered by the doorway. The noise of the horses came to them and they cursed loudly.

'They've got away. We'll never catch them on foot.'

'Yes we will – they're like all village dolts – sacks of meal on horseback.'

'But they say the gangly one's a whisperer – he can do anything with horses.'

'Except ride one. As for the brat—' a snort of laughter '—he'll never manage to cling on. It was hard going enough for him when we took them up to the holy well. Come on – I'll lay a bet we find them sprawled on their backsides within a mile of here.' The Bull snorted. 'We'll have our fun with them then, boys.'

'Alive, Richard says. We've to bring them back alive.'

'And so we will. Hey? We'll come back here later and finish off.'

I shivered at the sound of their laughter. I had one hand clamped over Ned's mouth and one over my own to stop the chattering of our teeth. I willed them to leave and they did. The noise of their going faded. I didn't think anyone had stayed behind but I waited until an owl hooted nearby and a badger grunted and rooted in the undergrowth next to us. Then I crept out.

They had gone but they would be back. Ned and me, we had to run, get away, but the night was bitter and we needed warmth and food or we would die. I had to go back into the hall. I had no choice.

'Stay here.' I slipped past the wall towards the door. Had they all gone? I listened. Not a sound. I eased the door open wider and crept inside.

All were dead. They were sprawled across the floor of the hall. Bryn's eyes were wide open and staring up to the open roof and the stars circling in the dark sky. Bogo was sliced open, like a carcass; his guts slithering on to the floor beside him. My lady was lying next to my lord and the child was face down a hand's reach away. I tried not to look at them. I grabbed for the rough-spun cloaks lying on the benches, and the last of the oatcakes and hard cheese I pushed into the pouch in my tunic. Bryn's broadsword was on the floor, without a stain, and I picked it up in two hands but it was too heavy for a skinny brat like me. Besides, it was almost as high as my armpits. His dagger was at his belt, though, the one he had held to my throat earlier that night: it seemed long ago. I took it. I knew he wouldn't mind.

A humped shape lay in a shadowy corner of the room. It was Llygad. Dark blood welled from his side and spilled on to the beaten earth of the floor. They had cut off his hands. I bent down and felt faint breath on my face. Not quite dead, then. I wanted to stroke his face and comfort him in his dying but I dared not. The *crwth* was near him, its bridge broken and its strings snapped but I couldn't bear to leave it there.

'I'll take the *crwth*, Llygad,' I whispered, willing him to hear me. 'We'll find Ieuan and tell him what has happened here. I swear it, Llygad.'

I was whimpering, fearful of the bloody room and the stench of death and the fierce men who lusted to kill Ned and me. The slightest of breaths on my cheek. A thread of voice.

'No fear. Cymer. Ieuan. '

Stumps where hands should be. A music man's hands.

'Go boy. Now.' His head lolled and his eyes glazed, sightless, unseeing.

I took the useless *crwth* and its bag and left him there. I went back to Ned, still crouching in the shadows where I had left him. I pulled one of the cloaks around him and fastened the pin.

'Come on, Ned, we have to go now.'

There was no sound as we crept out of the yard. I could not hear the night birds or the wind in the bare branches. I was listening for the Bull and his men but there was nothing. The mist had cleared, the half-moon was hanging in the sky and the stars were wheeling.

Seven

Stretch out your hand. Feel the sinews tighten and crack. Fingers splay like the points of a star. A crescent moon is hiding at the base of each nail. Curl your fingers into your hand, like a shell. Turn your hand palm uppermost. Your future is already written there in the lines crossing your palm. Infinity is in your hand. High above is the other infinity. Stars scatter and a crescent moon sickles God's hand.

The horses had scattered towards the east, to where the North Star hung fast. I thanked God for this, and for a sky blown clear of mist though the wind was icy. We had to go south west, and keep going through the night for as long as we were able. I scanned the stars. There were the Seven Sisters that Brother John called the Pleiades. And the bright eye of Aldebaran that was called the eye of the Bull, and there the Bull's huge head. I shuddered. The Bull was at our back. I stopped thinking. Sometimes thinking doesn't do you any good. Only keep the mind empty of everything but the noise of men and the way ahead. No thinking about the bloodshed inside the old hall, and the slaughtered bairn and my lord's head crushed. No thinking about my lady, the bright Angharad for whom Ieuan ap y Gof had made a praise song. No water to spring out of the ground where this lady fell. No saintly uncle to give back life.

My mind filled again with the sweeping arc and the shining edge of a sword hacking into the place where shoulder joined neck. The dreadful sound of iron on flesh. Dreadful choking as life left the body. Spurting blood, bright red. She dropped like a stone and her eyes, her bright, clear eyes, flashed towards heaven. All dead, all dead, and the stench of their blood in my nostrils and its taste in my mouth, like metal. I was shuddering with shock and fear and Ned shuddered with me. Thinking doesn't do you any good. Don't think.

I emptied my mind again and shifted my gaze from the Bull to Orion. There were the two stars that marked his shoulders, and the two that were his knees, and the three stars in the middle that were his belt, with a dagger hanging down from it. I felt at the dagger hanging from my belt and braced my shoulders and stiffened my knees. I would be Orion. I would be the hunter. I would find Ieuan ap y Gof and bring Ned to him, and the *crwth*, as I had sworn to Llygad. And I had sworn to Mam that I would look out for Ned. I pulled the cloak tighter about me and hitched it up about my middle. It was too big for me and even its warm rough cloth could not stop me shivering.

✝ You think it strange that a young boy should have these thoughts? Whistling in the dark, my friend, whistling in the dark. What else was there to do? If we had stayed, we would have died. We had to go on. No going back. This was war and the smell of death was everywhere. If strength came from the stars, wasn't that fitting?

'Come on, Ned.'

He was standing still, just where I had left him and his face was white like a ghost's and he was jerking and shaking.

'Ned!' I gripped his arms tight. 'Ned, come on. We have to go.'

His eyes swivelled towards the hall and back to me and they showed white as a frighted animal.

'We have to leave them, Ned. There's nothing we can do here. We have no choice. We must find Ieuan.' I said the name again. 'Ieuan, Ned – we must find him. We must go to Cymer to meet him. It is what my lady and my lord would wish. Look, Ned, I have the *crwth*. I swore to Llygad to bring the *crwth*.' I had wrapped it in its oiled bag and slung it across my back and I turned now to show Ned. But there was no grin and gurgle, no sign that he understood me, no flicker in his eyes at the mention of the music man's name.

I had to look out for him. I'd promised Mam. I'd been looking out for him all my life. That's what I'd thought. But now I knew it was Ned who had looked out for me. When I stumbled after him across the fen paths, it was Ned who led the way. When I fell in the dark pool, it was Ned who rescued me. It was Ned who knew the ways through marshland and woodland; Ned who crept silently through the abbey itself; Ned who had no fear of the dark. Now his soul had been driven out and his empty body shook and shivered as if with the ague. When he moved, it was like an old man. Now it was truly my turn to look out for him and bring him safely home.

The hall was built on a lip of ground on the hillside. We scrambled down, clinging to tree branches and roots. Below us was the rushing of water and the ground grew marshy but it was, after all, only a small stream flowing fast over rocks. On the far side the land rose steeply again, a great dark mass heavy against the dark sky, and I was thinking suddenly of that first night at Lincoln and the way the castle had loomed over us, shutting us in. That was long ago, another life.

The way was black as the blackest pools in the fens. Ned would have found the way, like a bat in the dark. I was blind, leading like a blind man. We struggled upwards, almost losing our foothold; the hurtle of hell into the dark places below. I put Ned's hand on my shoulder and made him keep it there. Once when I slipped he fell on top of me so that the breath was knocked out of my body and I lay in the wet grass with the stars swinging above us and no sound but our breath rasping. I waited until I could move again and heave both of us on to our feet. Then we were climbing up a bank and rolling and slithering down the other side into a ditch with another steep bank to climb. It was enough. Orion's knees were shaking and his shoulders sagging and Ned a dead weight at his side. The moon was tilting westward and its light showed huge boulders standing upright like men and a thorny tree leaning over them. We crept into their shelter, pitiful wretches, and dragged the comfort of the rough-spun cloaks around us. If we huddled together, we might find warmth enough.

I didn't expect to sleep but sorrow and sleep together held me in their grip. It was full daylight when I woke. The sky was bright blue and the ground sharp with frost. Our cloaks were white frozen and cracked when I moved. Cold stung my nose and throat when I breathed in and ghosted the air when I breathed out. I was lying against Ned. He was half sitting, his back propped against the rock and his eyes wide. For a spit of time I thought he had died in the night and my heart jerked. Then I felt his breath on my cheek and knew he was alive.

Carefully I crept out and gazed about me though there was little I could see. We were deep in a ditch. Frost clung to its sides and settled into its hollows. On either side the banks rose sharply and ran in an even bend. Above me was a third bank, its shoulders clear against the blue sky, and I knew all were man-made, just as I knew no man lived here now. This was an ancient fort built with cunning yet nothing was left but these banks and ditches tugged at by winds and hung with frost. It was a world laid waste. I wondered if there were ghosts here, crying out for what was right. I wondered if there had been a boy about my age trapped in a war that went on and on, and if he had seen blood spilt and innocents slaughtered.

High above two buzzards rode the air, mewing to each other, their sharp gaze fixed on the ground far below. One stooped in a swift dive and I wondered what small animal would be grasped in its keen claws. I was saddened for the thing and knew its fear, but my belly rumbled and I knew also the hunger the buzzards felt. How could it be right for the small things of this earth to be hunted and killed? Yet God made it happen: God the all-powerful, the all-knowing, the all-wise.

✝ That morning I thought God had forsaken me. Hell is desolation and I was desolate. Those good people – our enemies – dead, sprawling in their own black blood; Ned's soul drifted from his body; Dick Thatcher drowned; our friends from the village all gone. I was bereft of all that was dear. I was only a boy and life, that bright morning, was a dark place. And Bogo? Dead too. Did I count him friend or foe? My mind was full of whirring insects, my friend. Whirring insects. But what could you know of this? You have known only the safety of the cloister. No, no, I do not blame you. I envy you.

My body ached and my belly cried. I stretched and rubbed life into my tired arms and legs. My mouth watered at the thought of the oatcakes and hard cheese I had taken from the hall but I knew I must first climb the bank to the top. I must know if we were still safe from our hunters. I told Ned to stay where he was but I don't know if he heard me. His eyes fixed on nothing and drool dripped from the corner of his mouth. I wiped it away. Then I left him.

I climbed slowly on all fours, grunting like a swine. There was a gap in the bank; the way in, I was thinking, and I greeted the ghosts that were there. They were crowding me, asking for news, and I told them it was war and death, death and war, and heard their howls of grief. Or maybe I was near witless myself from shock and sadness.

Then I was on the brink of the hill in an open space. The tops of the banks kept me safe from sight though icy wind whipped my face and brought water to my eyes. I rubbed them and rubbed again. I stared and stared.

I could see the whole earth. I felt like the buzzard. Like Orion. Like – wicked thought – God. To the north there was the sea, glittering in streaks of silver and dark blue, and blue like periwinkle and green like new apple leaves. It was not like our northern sea, brown and grey. This was a cloth of light. Six boats bobbed near to the shore and one was further out, sails swelling in the free wind. Seagulls, dazzle-bright, flocked in its wake: a fishing boat hauling back the catch. I was thinking of the stinking brown mud of Flint and the ooze and slap of the river. The sea was so close. If we had been like birds flying high, not worms grubbing in the dung, we would have known.

To the west and south, hills; beyond them, mountains, range on range, already hooded with snow. This, then, was Llewelyn's land, and these mountains his stronghold. Small wonder he fought for it. Even then, cold and hungry and frightened almost out of my wits, my soul leaped at the sight of world on world, and blue sea beyond, and the beauty of it all. I was shivering with cold and fear, and my belly was aching with emptiness, but my soul gave thanks to God who had saved us from that night of horror.

Behind me, eastwards, the risen sun was lying low over the long line of hulking hills we had climbed in the dark. Beyond that, Flint, and beyond that, England and home. Our way home was taken from us. That way, Edward's wolves were sniffing out our tracks. Besides, we had chosen, back there in the hall. Ned had chosen. Now, our way was south-west to Cymer, towards the mountains, and Ieuan, and whatever God willed. I had sworn it.

I looked at the sea again and the wide river twisting towards it. Down there was Rhuddlan and Peter Long and Gil Allbone and the Northman and I longed to go to them and be comforted. They were grown men and I was just a boy. They would know what to do. They would take care of Ned.

It was the child whining. The other Will, hard knot for heart, knew they could not help. They were bound men and, if we went to them, it would be the worse for them and we would be taken anyway and killed. My guts twisted and I crouched to shit and groaned with pain.

It's only afterwards you see the choices you should have made. If Ned and I had not gone to the holy well; if Bryn and Islwyn had not taken us; if Ned had not played the *crwth*— Which of those 'ifs' began it all? If Llewelyn had not withheld his homage to Edward; if we had not been taken to Flint; if the music man had not come to the abbey— Like spiders' webs, thin as the shreds of the Virgin's shroud, our lives are woven from strands. It's not easy, choosing, and sometimes we have no choice.

Who is to blame for the death of the innocent?

I was thinking of the dark hall with no fire, no candle; no light. They had had no sending, God forgive me. I scrubbed my face with my knuckles. Grieving must come later. For now, Ned and me, we had a second life. Bogo and my lord and my lady had given us a second life.

I fixed my gaze on the nearer slopes, like the buzzard, searching for movement. There was none. Gorse burned against the sky and mist clung to pockets of the hills. Frost glittered. Nothing. I scrambled back down the bank to Ned. He was sitting where I had left him, still staring into nothingness. I took a flask of water and softened an oatcake and fed it to him, crumb by crumb. I tipped holy water into his mouth and watched his Adam's apple move up and down as he swallowed. I wiped his mouth and smoothed his hair with my hands and kissed his forehead.

'Come on, Ned, we have to go.'

I led him up the banks and through the fort and down the further side of the hill. The ground fell away steeply. We slithered down to a broad valley, clinging to winter grass and prickly gorse stems. Trees clustered at the bottom near a whitewashed chapel, bright as a star, and a scattering of hovels. I wondered if it was safe. There was no stench of burning, no sign of torching. We hid in the shelter of a dung heap. Hens scratched round us, not caring. I watched a woman drawing water from the river, hefting the buckets and slopping half the water. She should have been well set, like Mam, with strong arms, but her face was gaunt. An old man limped past without knowing we were there. A holy man hurried into the church. No children. I saw no children. No young men or women. Storm clouds heaped themselves over the mountains, hanging heavy until the bright sun was shut out. Freezing wind bit into us.

Hooves thudded and bridles chinked. I wasn't surprised when the King's men rode up the valley and into the village. The Bull wasn't with them but they had dogs. I burrowed us into the dung heap, grateful for its stench. At least it would cover our own. All the same, I fumbled for Bryn's dagger. The holy man came out of the church, his skirts flapping in the wind. He wrapped his hood more closely about him. The horsemen stopped and one of them leaned down to speak to him. He shook his head. I saw his lips shape, 'No. No one.' They were seeking us then. His lips moved again. 'Yes.' Or maybe it was, 'Bless.' It came to the same: there was no help here. I did not blame him, though he was a holy father. He had his church and what was left of his flock to look out for.

The men rode on, the dogs fanning out round them, whining and snuffing the ground. One came closer, ears pricked, red tongue lolling and breath rasping. Its eyes were red as the fiends on our church wall at home. My hand gripped tight hold of the dagger. The beast cocked its hind leg and steaming piss splattered the dung heap. One of the men turned back and barked an order; the dog shook itself and bounded after them. The holy father watched them out of sight before he turned back into the white church.

We waited until all was still, then we crept out. Beyond the church and the village was a stone bridge over the river. We scurried over as fast as Ned's crab gait let us. I dreaded the shout that meant we were seen but it didn't come. There was only the empty sound of the wind blowing through the valley like breath through a reed pipe. We followed a track heading out of the valley and into the cloud-hugging hills. Better to be a buzzard than a worm.

We kept clear of places where folk lived. We skirted a church tucked in a dip, and a crag of rock rearing over it and a farmstead close by. There was a crossroads and we went south-west. The day had turned dark and storm clouds billowed across the sky. Ahead of us was the darker shape of the high hills. When we came to a burnt-out farm we stopped. The stench of smoke lingered. Buildings and fields and stunted trees and the winter store were all scorched black. No sign of the folk whose home it was. I wondered if their bodies were lying somewhere, as charred and blackened as the beams fallen from the roof, but I didn't look for them. Instead, I made us a shelter of sorts against a stone wall that looked sound enough. We went hungry that night, with only the last scraps of hard cheese to fill our bellies. My body was bruised with cold but it was my heart that hurt most. I longed for Ned to come back to his body. I drifted and dozed and jerked awake at every rustle and creak. If I slept, I dreamed of the Bull travelling the skies to seek us out, his great eye glaring. I dreamed I saw him stoop and pounce and woke trembling.

The morning was dull and drear. The sky was flint-flake over land that rose higher and higher. Rising or not, it was water bound, with dips of dark pools hidden in bracken. Our feet and legs were sodden and our bodies chilled through long before the wan sun waned. All about us was desolation. I didn't know what was north or south or east or west. All I knew was lifting one foot, another foot, heaving Ned with me, watching out for the dark pools of freezing water and trailing roots. Squalls of icy wind whipped us on our way and knocked the breath out of us. Hard hail turned to snow that settled on our bodies and frosted our faces. We were snow men swallowed up in a white, whirling world. I knew what happened to men caught in weather like this…

They never knew who the wayfarer was. Peter Long had seen him passing through the village and urged him to stop the night but he would not. The boy's father found him next morning out on the marsh. He was huddled into his journeying cloak, sitting under reeds as stiff and white as the man himself.

'Gone on a longer journey than he reckoned,' Peter Long said when he knew.

'All wrapped up ready for it in a white shroud. That's what it looked like when me and the boy found him.'

'Halfwit. Should have taken shelter, bitter night like that,' said John Thatcher.

I stumbled over stones, ankle high, and we both fell. I cracked my cheek against something sharp hidden under thin snow. I was sobbing for breath, crawling on hands and knees and dragging Ned with me. I wasn't frightened. I was angry. I heard myself shouting at God that Ned was no sinner. I might be, but not Ned. He didn't deserve this punishment. He was a hunched heron, wise above all others. He was not one of those spotted with evil that killed with a single leap and feasted on the still-living body. Those were the brutes that did not deserve God's love and forgiveness. Ned did. But there was nobody to hear me in that wilderness, not even God, and my voice was whipped away by the wind.

We were tumbling again down into a narrow grave. God's joke, I was thinking, or God's anger? Then I saw it was a passage lined with stones standing like men. It led to a room, stone built and stone roofed and out of the worst of the wind and the blinding snow. A miracle. I huddled Ned close and tried to rub warmth and life into him but he was chilled through and through and slumped unseeing, unmoving. My fingers caught the hard edge of the swan pipe. I tugged it out. I raised it to my mouth and blew into it but only a hiss of breath came out between my lips. I knew it wouldn't sing for me. It needed Ned to do that. Without him there was no song. I felt numb, body and soul, and wondered if this was the cold sickness and if we were going to die after all. I choked back my anger and tried to pray. Then I wrapped the cloaks round us both though they were wet enough, God knew, and little comfort.

I suppose I must have fallen asleep.

A brave fire was flickering warmth. I could see men gathered about a glowing hearth just outside the passage. The flames leaped high into the night sky and shed light on the walls and on their faces and long beards. The men looked towards us and I was comforted by their grave, calm faces. There was no danger here. The snowstorm had passed. The sky was clear and the stars bright. I counted the Pleiades. No sign of the Bull. I wanted to rouse Ned but I couldn't. I felt warm and my eyes were heavy and I slept again.

Waking was hard. Ned was leaning hard against me, fast asleep. I was glad for him and eased him back against the wall. It was barely light. Snow had drifted into the room and I saw now it was just stones stood upright with a great stone laid across for a roof. Through the opening I could see the land was snow wrapt and the sky lowering with threat of more to come. I struggled to stand upright, my head almost touching the stone ceiling. The stones stared at me, as full of faces as the shouting trees, and I laughed. My head felt light and free and I was thinking it was with hunger and gladness that we were not dead. I walked out into snow that crunched underfoot. My eyes watered with its brightness. We were between two low crags. Mountains lay to the north, their high tops lost in snow and cloud. Slanting below us was marshland and reeds. I looked again towards the nearer crag and felt a fluttering of fear. Smoke. A rough-built hovel crouched next to a holly tree bright with berries. Even as I looked, the door pushed back and an old man came out, stooping under the lintel. He straightened, a tall man girded with thick woollens. His beard was long and tangled, like the men in the night, and streaked like the coat of a brindled dog. He looked to where I stood, shielding his eyes from a sun that lurked low under heavy skies. I waited. He walked towards me, slowly, through the snow, his prints dark in its whiteness.

'Welcome, young friend.' He spoke in Welsh and I answered in the same language.

'It was a bad night for wayfarers to be out. If I'd known, you'd have taken shelter with me.'

'But you knew we were here,' I blurted. 'I saw you.'

His eyes fixed on me, a young man's eyes in an old man's body, bright like the mead Jack the Brewer made. 'You saw me? When?'

'Last night. You were at the fire. Over there.'

'What fire?'

'Over there. Outside the rock room.' We looked. The snow was smooth. No trace of ash or smouldered branches. 'It was there,' I said.

'Maybe you were dreaming of fire. It's been known.'

I wished then I had held my tongue but it was too late. I thought of Bryn's dagger left in the rock room; of Ned, asleep and helpless; of the broken *crwth* that I had promised to take to Ieuan. 'There was a fire and I saw you,' I said again but my voice was small, like a young boy's. 'There were others with you. Where are they?' Maybe they were waiting for us, hidden behind the crags or lurking in the hovel. I clenched my fists, getting ready to swing them, to hit as hard as I could and run back to Ned. Maybe we could still escape.

'My boy, there are no others. I'm the only living soul in this place.' His teeth gleamed like fangs behind his beard. I glared at him. 'And the dead won't harm you, that's for sure. You're safe enough here. Now, breakfast. Are you hungry?' He was smiling. Not fangs at all.

Was I hungry? I started towards him then stopped. I glanced back towards the rock house.

'Got someone with you? Bring him along as well.' When I didn't move he shrugged his thin shoulders and tut-tutted and raised his hands up to God. 'Bless you, boy, what a to-do. You've no cause to be frightened by old Derw. There's nobody comes here that matters. That's because there's nobody here that matters.' He chuckled to himself. 'So – breakfast?'

I nodded. 'My brother—'

'Well, go and get him, boy.'

'He's not well. Not sick but—'

'Not himself, maybe?'

'No. Not himself.' I turned away before tears bleared my sight. 'I'll get him.'

'Come up to the home. Now if it's fire you're after, I've a good 'un going on the hearth. Good kindling, good wood – makes all the difference. Get your clothes bone dry before you know it.'

Ned was still drowsing. I shook him awake.

His eyes opened; those black eyes that used to be bright were dulled now. He'd black stubble about his face. I couldn't remember seeing it before. His thatch of hair was grown long and matted. He looked like a hunted animal. I was thinking about myself, a short, skinny brat with lank brown hair, fierce eyes and a scowling mouth. I wondered what the old man had seen.

'Ned, time to wake up. Time to eat. Come on now.'

Ned's eyes fixed on me. His mouth moved. He was gaping like a landed fish. I heard a gagging, gasping deep in his throat as he struggled to use his voice. 'Oh Ned. It's all right, Ned. It's going to be all right. We'll find Ieuan, Ned, and then it will be all right again. You'll see.' I wiped the snot and the tears from my face. I hugged him again and again. 'Now come on. We just have to go a bit across the way and there's an old man has breakfast for us. His name's Derw. Come on, Ned.'

He came gladly enough out of the rock room and stood blinking in the bright light of the snow. I led him back across my snow tracks to the hovel. Derw came out to us, long and thin like a dried eel. He was wiping his hands on his clothes.

'Good, good. Come in now, into the warmth.' He shepherded us over the threshold. I stood for a moment, waiting for my eyes to grow used to the dimness of a room without windows. There was a fug of warmth from the fire, held safe in its clay hearth, and smoke rising to the gap in the roof reeds. 'Take off your cloaks – look, hang them here where they'll dry out a treat. Sit down by the hearth. Pull your stools up close and warm yourselves through. You've had a cold night of it, that's for sure. Lucky to be alive. Now, let me see. Watch the porridge now. Don't let it catch. I'll see about bowls.'

He was talking more to himself than to us. I sat there in a blur of warmth, half listening to the rattle of pots behind me, sniffing up the smells coming from the porridge pot slung over the fire. I let the blaze of the fire warm me through. My toes and fingers tingled and ached. I held them out and watched the fire and the pot through my spread fingers. Ned was sitting hunched forward almost over the flames as if to get as close as he could to the heat of them. I kept my eye on him in case he should topple.

'Here now – get this inside you, boys.' Two bowls of steaming porridge. I grasped the spoon he gave me, my fingers stiff and awkward. The wooden spoon thunked on the wooden bowl as I dipped and lifted the porridge to my mouth. It was burning hot.

'Blow on it, blow on it. You'll burn your insides else.'

Had anything ever tasted so good? I tongued the grains in my mouth, felt the warm path it made down to my belly. I wanted to cram it all in at once and stop the aching emptiness. I didn't. I put my bowl down and picked up Ned's, blowing on the steaming spoonful I held to his mouth.

'Come on, Ned. It's warm. It's good.'

'Now, boy, let me do that. You get on with your own. Here now, Ned, eat up.'

And the old man fed Ned, spoonful by spoonful, blowing to cool the porridge and coaxing Ned to take another spoonful and another, waiting each time until Ned had gulped and swallowed. Once, Derw glanced at me and my empty bowl. 'Help yourself to more. One bowl's not enough for a growing boy, is it now?'

When Ned had swallowed the last of his, Derw went away and came back with two beakers brimful of something hot and honey-sweet.

'*Melissa officinalis* sweetened with honey. Good to ward off chills and settle the nerves.' My head jerked up at the Latin, and a herb-man's learning. He tut-tutted. 'What a boy you are for the startles. Nothing but lemon balm, boy, lemon balm – do you good.'

'Are you a holy man?'

'I wouldn't know about that. The village people bring me food from time to time. For the medicines, see. There are many useful plants that grow around here.' He chuckled to himself again. 'The villagers seem to think I'm some sort of holy man.'

'Have you always lived here?'

'Not always. I came across this place much as you did, one winter's night. That was many years ago now, when I was a young man.' He bent over the log pile and heaped his arms full. He came back to the hearth and carefully stacked the logs on to the glowing fire. 'I was sad at heart, much like you. I'd been away over the seas, fighting in the Crusades, see. Came back to find my family slaughtered and my home burnt to the ground.' He didn't look at me. He kept his gaze on the logs and the fire. 'I wandered for long enough before I found this place. I found peace here.'

I said nothing. He sat back on his heels. 'Tell me—'

I stiffened, waiting for the questions: who we were, where we'd come from. We'd shared his food and his hearth. He had a right to ask.

'I'd like to know about the fire; about those others.'

I let my breath go. 'Don't you want to know who we are?'

'I know who you are: two young wayfarers caught in the snow and, thanks to the gods, you're alive and well. I'm more interested in your dream, now.'

'Gods,' he said, but it didn't make its mark then.

'It wasn't a dream.' I stopped. It seemed unlikely, now, in the snowy morning with hot food in my belly. Even the terrors of the last days seemed like a dream. 'It must have been,' I muttered. 'Like you said, there was no fire.'

'But it seemed real?'

'Yes.' I shut my mouth. I wasn't going to play the halfwit for anybody, not even this old man who had fed and warmed us.

'Dream or vision, boy, I'd like to hear tell of it.' I looked up at him then.

'Vision?'

'Why not?'

That seemed less likely than anything. Holy men had visions, not skinny, mouthy brats.

'Yes, boy, vision. This has been a sacred place for many, many years. For more years than you can imagine. That place you call the rock room is the bone place of the old ones.'

I was thinking of the stone faces shouting joy. 'Do ghosts sleep there?'

'Maybe. I've seen nothing but I feel their presence.' His teeth showed again but this time I saw it straightaway as a smile. He stretched out a hand and smoothed Ned's tangled hair. 'I look after this place. There is nothing to fear.'

'I wasn't afraid.'

He chuckled. 'Are you frightened of anything, boy?'

I wriggled. 'Some things.'

'But not the ghosts of the old ones?'

'It seemed to me they were kind. They wanted to look after us.'

'Yes, boy, I think so.' He gazed into the fire. 'Did you hear anything? Did you hear the fire crackle or men's voices?'

I shook my head. There had been no sound. I frowned. 'Yes, there was something.'

I was thinking, thinking. It was no use.

'I can't remember. Not the fire or the men. Something.' I felt shame. 'I went back to sleep.'

'Good, good. That was what you needed. You and your brother.'

I looked down at Ned drowsing before the fire. 'Will he ever be well again?'

'Yes, I'm sure of it.' He looked for words. 'I think you've had hard times.'

It was easy, then, to tell him what had happened. I think I wept. Afterwards, I fell asleep again and when I woke I was huddled in the blankets that were Derw's bed. There was more food – rabbit stew, I think it was, with winter roots. Our bellies were full and we were warm and dry and I didn't want to leave this place. Outside, the snow had half melted in winter sun but clouds were pushing up over the mountains. Not long before the sky was black and dark closed in.

'How far to Gwytherin?' I asked.

'Not far – a step over the hill and down the cwm. The track is good if you follow the posts – keep close to them, now, no straying.'

'We can get there by nightfall, then?'

'Not even half a day's walk – if that's what you want, boy? You're welcome to stay, take pot luck for supper.'

I sighed. 'We must go.'

He nodded, knowing my mind. 'There's food to take with you and medicines – and supplies for Father John at Gwytherin. He's a good man – no need to fear him. He'll take care of you tonight and set you on the way for Cymer tomorrow, if the weather holds. If it's wild, stay where you are. No one will be stirring if bad weather comes, that you can be sure of.'

'What about you?'

'Me? Oh, I stay here, boy. If I don't look after the tomb, who will? They're all too busy filling graves with new dead these days to care about the old ones.'

'They say Llewelyn will surrender.'

'Maybe he will. The year turns, boy, and the seasons come and go. It will all go on, whether Llewelyn surrenders or not. Those mountains will be here long after we've left this life. The sea will batter the shore. There will be rain and snow and driving wind and the warmth of the sun, and we'll not be here to see it.' He chuckled, as if it did not worry him. And maybe it didn't. 'Come now, no time to waste if it's today you travel. I'll go a way with you, set you straight on the track.'

He walked with us a long stretch up the valley and on to the open moor. There he left us.

'May the gods go with you,' he said.

Yes, he said 'gods'. I hadn't misheard him. Since then I've travelled amongst men who worship other gods with as much fervour as we believe in and worship God and his Son who died for us and Mother Mary. Good men, like old Derw. Who is to say who is right and who is wrong? It seems to me it's the same but not the same, and we would do well to honour those other gods, and the folk who worship them.

I went back, you know, after the second war, after the Prince was murdered and Dafydd his brother slaughtered so cruelly. The land was blackened and holy places desecrated. Holywell was ruined. The Leopard made sure, that time, there'd be no more uprising. Derw was still there in his quiet corner, still tending the tomb. As he said, no one who mattered came there and no one was there who mattered. And who is to say if he got the last part right way round? A good man.

Mountains loomed ahead of us, fold on fold. All was bleak and cheerless. Behind us was Snowdon, where the Prince was trapped with his men. We trudged over the high ridge keeping close to the waymarkers. We were the only two creatures moving on the face of the earth. The sun, when we could see it, was a pale circle behind fast-moving cloud. No sound but our breathing cold air in through our nostrils and out through our mouths. Our eyes stung and watered with cold and our ears were reddened despite us pulling our hoods close round us. Today though, I knew the way to follow. We had dry clothes and food in our bellies, thanks to Derw. More than anything, hope was flickering. We were alive. We had survived this far. God hadn't forsaken us.

The track dropped down steeply. Snow had piled in the hollows and the going was harder than it had been up on the top. Light was fading and at first we didn't spot the white church against the white snow.

As Derw had promised, Father John was a good man, glad to have the gift of medicines and glad to give us shelter. If he wondered whether we sheltered from the winter night or from Edward's men, or Llewelyn's, he didn't say and didn't ask.

That was our fifth night, and the most comfortable. We were warm and our bellies full. Best of all, we were snug under thatch in the Father's house by Winifrede's church. Though her bones were long gone, taken to the abbey at Shrewsbury, her spirit was still in the place. I was thinking about Holywell, and how three times' asking would grant the prayer. Maybe, if I prayed in this place where she had been buried, it would count as a third time. So I prayed again to keep Ned safe and bring him home.

In the morning the weather had turned around. Frost glittered on grass and branches. Over Snowdon, clouds piled heavy but we were under blue sky. 'And, with God's grace, you should have fair weather for most of the day,' said Father John. He stopped by one of the two old yew trees that grew in the circle of the churchyard, their trunks already hollow with age. He lifted one of the berried branches.

'They say Winifrede herself planted these. They are witnesses to her miracle. I'm trying to grow more.' There were four stones standing in a row close by, like men-at-arms, and one with marks that looked like Latin writing. Old graves, said Father John, from Winifrede's time, but I was thinking of the bone house we had sheltered in. These were the stones of the old people standing in the churchyard, their gods with our God. I was thinking, then, about Derw and his care for the old ones and how things went on and on and how small we all were. Still, I pocketed a handful of the bright yew berries. If they were Winifrede's, maybe this was her blessing. If not, *Taxus baccata* was a strong poison and a weapon was a weapon. I looked at Ned standing idiot-like, mouth half-open and spit drooling. I wiped it away. I didn't like to see it. It reminded me of Tom Halfwit who lived just outside our village with his widowed mother. The village children used to tease him to anger until Ned stopped them.

'God be with you,' said Father John. 'Give my greeting to

Father Pedr.'

We were alone again but with the memory of warmth and care and knowing there was safe lodging that night. What do I remember of it now? Keen wind and black snow clouds at our backs gusting from the north; a man and his boy staggering homeward with bundles of branches and twigs, their faces wind roughened and sharp with mistrust; hoof beats ringing and us hiding until Edward's soldiers passed us by. Then knocking at a door and being let in; food and drink and no questions asked and set on our way next morning over bleak heath land.

It must have been the old stone road Bryn had spoken of, set stones still showing, sometimes overgrown, but a straight way. We came to a crossroads where we could see the lines of an old fort and what was left of buildings. High in the middle was a motte, steep-sided like a pudding bowl with a crust of snow. Most of the castle walls were gone, taken by stone robbers. Who could blame them, poor wretches? They had more need of good, shaped stone in this chill country than any ghosts. Blood freezing wind whistled through the gap in the high hills. There was fear here, and loneliness. We didn't stay but hurried on, and I was glad at last that ice had hardened marshland, making our way firm.

Then a stretch of oak trees, leafless in the nakedness of winter, frosted lichen hanging from great bleached boughs that writhed like the serpents in Father John's bestiary; birch trees with their ghost bark; dull bracken that hadn't died back, silvered where frost touched it; sly net of bramble looping across our path and everywhere sharp outcrops of grey rock with snow lodged under their ridges and drifting across open ground. We followed the river, as we'd been told. It rushed through rock to where it joined with another river. Here were the falls Father Pedr had told us of; we were on abbey grounds now. He'd told us, too, how we'd to mind our footing. If we hurried, we'd be at the abbey by nightfall. 'No lingering in the forest,' he warned. 'It's not safe. Lawless, these days, and gold tempts all men, even though the abbey holds the rights to mine there. God willing, there'll be peace again soon.'

It sounded like thunder. It was not from the sky but from water pounding, flashing; thrusting from high above us to fall headlong over rocks into a frothing, swirling, black kettle. We stood on its edge, my mouth dropping open like Ned's, catching flung spray. I watched the swirl of water in the black bowl, and the way it hurled itself into its new path, white water turning over and over and dragging with it tree trunks and branches and shifting stones, and rushing on through a cleft in the rocks. A second fall thundered away to our left, just within sight, falling from ledge to ledge into a sullen black pool and out through rocks to where the waters met.

The noise was deafening; it hammered in my ears.

What was it that warned me? Half heard shrill warning of a blackbird? Sharp crack of a trodden branch? I spun round.

Three men, hoods pulled well over their heads, carrying axes. This I saw in a flash before I stepped back, lost my footing and slithered over the edge towards the pounding water. It was Ned who stopped me, Ned's hand that shot out and grasped my wrist, hauled me back to safety, pushed me on to safe ground; let me go because he was falling, falling. I was on my knees, screaming his name above the crashing water. I hardly remember what I did next. I was mad with terror. I think I scrambled down the rocks by the side of the spray-flung fall and waded out into the swirling water, clinging to any handhold there was. I saw Ned's head bobbing above the water then his body, caught like the branches against the rocks before he was swirled again into the path of the river. I slipped on slimy stones and was flung into the icy water and felt its greedy drag before it hurled me against rough rock. I was winded, gulping air, gasping with the shock of the water's coldness. My lips were numbed and my scalp screamed. I thrashed like a landed mullet. Where was Ned? Was he, too, wrapped about in this icy wetness or had he been, God willing, thrown ashore? The rush and roar of the waters drowned my senses and filled my nostrils and ears and mouth. I was gulping icy water now, not air, still calling Ned's name but the sound buckled and bubbled. Then hands were hauling me back. I fought them off, coughing and choking, still trying to howl Ned's name.

'Lie still now – no need to waken the dead, brat,' a voice muttered.

Not dead. Not dead. My heart was bursting. Please God, don't let him be dead.

'Any luck, boyo?'

'He's fetched up on the bank – I'll go down and see but it'll be a miracle if he's lived through that. What about this one?'

'Alive – just.' A grim voice. 'Soaked through and his head's bashed in. Broken arm, maybe. Too shocked yet to feel pain.'

'Or give us any bother. What's he carrying in the bag, now? Anything worth having?'

'A *crwth*. Damaged but a good one. Lucky it didn't go with him into the water.'

'Doesn't look much like a bard, does he now? D'you think he pinched it?'

I heard it all in a haze, my head lolling against cold rock. So they would kill me. If Ned was dead, it didn't matter what happened to me. So near to Cymer and Ieuan. God was cruel.

A low call from across the river. 'This one looks done for. Shall I let him lie?'

'No. Take 'em both up. Best get them to the abbey.'

'To the abbey? Have you lost your wits? There'll be questions, boy.'

'We can't leave the poor devils here.'

'You and your conscience, Dic – you'll be the death of us.'

'Talking of death, looks like two corpses we'll be bringing in,' I heard one of them say but I was slithering to the ground by then.

Eight

Trace the shape of a triangle in the palm of your hand. Now observe how that roof end makes the same shape. And tonight, when the bright stars show themselves, see the triangles formed in the everlasting firmament. All are the same; all are triangles, whatever their size, wherever they are. So with music; whether it is music played on an instrument or the music that resonates between body and soul or music made by the cosmos itself: all sound the same note. It is ratio that joins together the concord of sounds, like the weights of the hammers in the smithy. Ratio is logos. In the beginning was logos.

Warmth. Well-being. Bliss. Somewhere the sound of the stars themselves. Sleep, forever and ever.

A voice, droning on and on, the words out of hearing, buzzing like a gnat.

Eyes heavy, weighted. Too heavy to lift. Warmth and comfort, but for the droning voice. Is he dead? Is he dead? Kill the gnat. Sleep. Gentle music. Was I buried with the old ones in the bone cave?

A touch on the mouth. *Drink, Will. Not dead. Not dead. Sleep.*

The voice, droning. I wished it would stop. I wanted to hear the music. Eyes forced open. White, white everywhere. Was this the snow death?

Ned's pale face hanging over mine.

'Are we dead?' A croak.

Ned's fingers stroking my forehead, smoothing my eyes. Sleep. Sleep.

The boy woke to a white room and clean bed covers pulled tight around him. There was a faint scent of lavender, like a summer afternoon. Outside the window, the leaves of a tree lifted and fell and sighed and their shadows filtered the sunlight and flickered on the white walls in moving patterns. The boy frowned. Where was he? He remembered helping with the thatching and the jolt when his foot slipped, and falling helplessly to the ground. The snap of broken bone. Pain. Nothing. Waking in the abbey infirmary and Ned sitting by the side of his bed. Father John fussing, bringing him a drink of something sweetened with honey that sent the pain away. Peace and comfort, far away from Mam's sharp tongue and hard hand.

Waking to a white room. I blinked.

'Where am I?'

'With friends.'

'Ned?'

'Alive and well, child, and doing his share of keeping you alive.'

My throat ached. My voice was hoarse.

'You've done nothing but talk for days without end. Quiet now. Drink this.'

'Ned?'

But I was asleep.

When I woke again, winter sun was shining low through an arched window on to my bed and my face. My eyes were dazzled. A shape crossed between me and the sun. Ned, pale and weary but alive. I wanted to thank God who had brought us safe here but I thought of my anger against him and guilt kept me silent.

The men in the wood had a barrow – very handy for collecting kindling, they told Father Abbot – so they'd laid us both in it and brought us straight to the abbey, more dead than alive.

'If it was grains of gold they found, they well deserved it,' said Brother Ifor who served in the infirmary. 'A long way it was they had to bring you. Easy for them to pass you by and leave you for dead. But they didn't, and God will remember them for this.'

Ieuan knew us straight away. Abbot Llewelyn had us carried to the infirmary and there I had lain for days, shouting myself hoarse. 'It was great fear we had for you, child,' said Brother Ifor. 'Nonsense it was you were gabbling until we thought you'd be talking yourself into your grave.'

Ned had gained strength more quickly. Maybe the tumbling in the cold waters of the river had brought him to his senses. Maybe it was the sight of Ieuan. Maybe it was because he needed to help me. Whatever the way, he sat by me and played and played sweet music on the swan pipe: music to heal the hurts of soul and body. Not the *crwth*. He wouldn't touch the *crwth*. There was no grinning now. His face was sad and his dark eyes no longer bright but his soul was back in his body, and his wits in his head.

And there was Ieuan ap y Gof, fiery-red hair damped down with ashy grey. The forefingers of his playing hand were stiff and unbending, like the broken wings of a bird. Or a fallen angel.

'Badly set, I fear.' He stretched out his hand, palm uppermost. A puckered white scar sickled its middle. When Dolforwyn was taken, friends helped him escape but his leg, the broken leg that had kept him all winter at our abbey, was still weak. He had fallen heavily; his hand was smashed and ripped and there was no one to mend it until he got to Cymer. 'I had news of Gwydion. Little better than a prisoner; a caged songbird, poor boy. But alive, young Will, alive, hey?'

We were alive, yes, but I was thinking of those others and the blood spilt and how it was hard to understand why wrongdoers lived and the innocent died. It's not easy, choosing. I wondered if God found it hard to choose – if he ever made the wrong choice. But that was a wicked thought and I dare not tell it to anyone. It seemed to me I was full of wickedness. What if it were my choices that had brought them death? I had time, now, to think of this, lying in the clean bed in the abbey's infirmary. I should have stopped Ned from going to the well that night. Peter Long and the Northman had warned me to take care; we were being watched; we were being followed. They must have followed us to the holy well and then tracked us to the old hall and slaughtered those good people and the bairn. The thought lay on me, as heavy as the timbers that crushed Dick Thatcher.

A sweet song that praised a maid's beauty.

All the peace and harmony that was between us shattered.

Her eyes, her eyes of immortal brightness, round and round they came and flashed towards heaven.

No water to spring out of the ground where this lady fell. No saintly uncle to give back life.

'The *crwth*?' I said. I was still croaking words.

'You did well, boy, very well. It's safe. Dic handed it over to Father Abbot – Llewelyn, his name, like our Prince – and he gave it to me.'

'He's dead.' I didn't name him. There was no need.

'Yes. I knew as soon as I saw the *crwth*. Poor Llygad. At least I have my life and my hands but neither of us will make music again. Not only that, boy. It's over. Of course, you don't know. Llewelyn surrendered. The Treaty was signed a week ago, handing over his rights and most of his lands. We're at peace, boy.' His voice was bitter.

✝ A date that will be remembered for ever and ever, though few will sing of it: 9 November 1277. While Ned and I were drowning in the falls of the Mawddach, the Treaty of Aberconwy was signed and Bishop Anian of St Asaph released Llewelyn ap Gruffudd, the last Prince, from the hell of excommunication and admitted him back into the Holy Church and the hope of salvation. His wedding to Eleanor, daughter of Simon de Montfort, was already being talked of, planned for St Edward's Day, in England, in great state, with Edward's blessing, both saint's and king's. You could say Edward stole that day from Llewelyn, too, if you were minded. He humbled our prince with his royal magnanimity.

New beginnings, new beginnings, wouldn't you say? And the man deserved his bride, God knows. At his age, and a life of fighting, he deserved a wife to take to his bed and the comfort of children – though there was but the one daughter and little comfort to be had from wife or child, poor Prince, if he'd but known. But that November it seemed all might yet be well, since the wounded lion had swallowed his pride and the leopard sheathed his claws.

It should have been new beginnings for Ned and me, as well, at Cymer. 'Where the waters meet': that's the meaning, in the Welsh tongue, and it was where the river Mawddach met the Wnion and flowed down the estuary to the sea. It was a Cistercian house of the white brothers, like our abbey; the same but not the same. Being there was like the eight note: the first note miraculously repeated but at a different pitch. That's what Ieuan ap y Gof said.

Not much of a miracle for me, not at first. Every night I was fretting and fussing and twisting and tossing and belabouring myself for my sins until poor Brother Ifor was beside himself with worry. Poor man. A good man. An innocent who lost his life in the second war. Ah well.

'Brother Ifor tells me you suffer from night terrors,' said Ieuan ap y Gof. He came softly into the room, a slight man with stooped shoulders and the fire of his hair pale now as penitence, but he snapped the stillness of the winter day with his coming. 'A sad case of guilty conscience, from what he can tell from your ravings.'

My mouth was dust dry; I couldn't utter a sound. If I'd tried, I'd have gurgled like Ned.

'Tongue tied at last, Will?'

I nodded. He was stern, his eyes blue as a wintry sky. He held Llygad's *crwth* in his good hand and his own slung over his back. 'Come now, you and Ned. Llygad's *crwth* is repaired and it's time you were as well. Enough of this whipping yourselves with guilt and sadness. Tell me, young Will, what has happened to burden you with such guilt?'

I stared through him. Blood, blood, and eyes staring to heaven. Llygad's hands lying limp on the hall floor, fingers curling, and stumps at the ends of his arms. My lady and my lord, both dead. The bairn. I shut my eyes tight but I could see them still.

'They were my *teulu*, remember. It is my loss, too.'

I said bitterly, 'It was my doing, their deaths.'

'How can that be?'

In my head I saw the silent hall, and the bodies, and splashes of red blood like wine. Then it was jumbled with tumbled barges and men drowning and a buzzard prowling on the updraft. Out it all came; I couldn't stop, even though Ned was crouching by my side and I could feel him shivering and I feared his wits would scatter again. 'If He's God, why did He let it happen?' Ned's teeth started to clatter in his head. I grabbed his hands and held them tight between my own; 'It's all right. We're safe, Ned, safe.'

I dare not look at Ieuan ap y Gof. He was still as a stone.

'Why did He let it happen?' he said at last. He sighed, shrugged. 'Who can say, Will? There are men of our time who ponder this question. They agonise as you do. They risk excommunication because they challenge the Church and God Himself.' He sighed again. 'I have no answer for you, Will. The good father would no doubt tell you we cannot see God's great plan. It's a question of faith, and a leap of faith. It is believing that all will be well because God wills it so.'

I didn't answer. I huddled in the blankets.

'Why did you let it happen?' He was silent and so was I. I waited. 'You think you are so important, Will? You think you make things happen?' I cringed. 'How are you to blame?'

'Because I—'

'Oh yes. You have said. You should have stopped Ned. Not gone to the holy well. You knew the Bull watched you.'

I shivered under the blankets. His voice was cold, damning. He lifted his hurt hand, swept it to one side, wiping out my stuttering.

'Think, Will. Why were they travelling, my Lord and the Lady Angharad? To find me. Is it then my fault they died? Think again, Will: I escaped Dolforwyn but Gwydion was taken. Is this also my fault?'

He stopped. I murmured something. He spoke again, not listening to me, maybe not even talking to me.

'Is truth a single harmony? You may as well ask why Llewelyn chose not to pay homage to the King. Was it then the Prince himself who started this accursed war? Or did it lie deeper, in Edward's nature? Who can tell where it starts? It is like the old carvings of the serpent, twisting and turning until it bites its own tail.' He laughed, short and sharp. 'Boethius, that great man, knew this hundreds of years before you were born. "Each life to its own purpose clings; and yet the flesh-entangled soul cannot see the subtle links that bind the whole."'

Again his voice stopped. I shot a look at him. He was gazing out of the window, his teeth gnawing at his bottom lip, and I was afraid though I did not know why. Outside, clouds heaped and gathered over the mountains.

'Will, have you ever asked yourself why I was there in your abbey?'

'Your broken leg?'

'There were other places I could have sheltered and mended.'

'To find out what the King was going to do?' I whispered.

'Most of that we already knew.'

Snow began to fall quietly, shadowy outside the window. Inside, the fire crackled and leapt up its chimney and the flickering made strange shapes on the walls of the room. Ieuan ap y Gof turned from the window and fixed his eyes on us. I was sitting up in the bed, hugging my knees. Ned was coiled close to me and he had pulled one of the blankets tight around us both. I could feel the warmth of his body, and his breath came soft on my cheek. Ieuan ap y Gof watched us a moment longer and then he smiled as if the sight of us pleased him.

'Enough of soul searching. This is just the dreary winter's afternoon for a story, don't you think?'

I sighed and nodded, settled back into my blankets and eased my splinted arm. Beside me, Ned shifted and stretched, and folded his body into itself.

'This is a story of great love and great sacrifice. It is a story that has waited a long time to be told.'

While he was speaking, he had unslung his *crwth* and held it now cradled on his lap, resting against his hurt hand. With his good hand he plucked the strings so that whispers breathed into the shadowy corners of the fire-lit room and his voice fell into the lilt of the storyteller.

'Listen now. Once upon a time – that is the way stories begin, Will, isn't it?

'Once upon a time there was a man, Meurig ap Dafydd, lord of lands between the sea and the mountains. Door of oak he was, swift and fierce in battle as a falcon. But it was his fate to be winged by an English arrow and be taken prisoner by an English knight. He was held captive in a moated hall far away from his own land and his own people and he pined there for its sea-coast and its mountains, its woods and homesteads and wild wilderness.

'The English knight had in his service a man-at-arms, devoted and loyal. And this man had two daughters. The elder was the woman of the house, had been since their mother died. She was a plain, brown girl, sharp-tongued at times, if truth were known: a soldier's daughter. The younger was a lovely girl, pale and slender, a dreamer who loved stories and music. She was her father's treasure.

'And the treasure, too, of the older sister. This is no fairy tale, no wicked sister and beautiful heroine. The younger girl was loved by father and sister, and was loving in return.

'She pitied the fettered falcon caught in his cage. She sighed to hear the tale of his courage and wept to hear of his wounds and his capture. How did they meet and exchange vows of love? Who knows? Love works its own magic. Enough to say they did meet, and the proof of that was in her swelling belly.

She hid it from her father but impossible to hide it from the sister.

'It was the older sister who helped the falcon to flight. He escaped to his own country promising to come back but there was still war between the two countries and he never returned. Years later, he married but his marriage was barren. Later still, he was grievously wounded in battle and died.

'And the girl? When she was but eight months gone, she gave birth to a boy with eyes bright and dark as his father's. And the girl died, begging her sister to care for the child as if he were her own.

'And the older sister, plain, brown girl, soldier's daughter, loyal and true, gave her oath. She loved her sister. She had no choice, if the babe was to live. Who else would look out for the child? She braved her father's anger and grief; she found herself a husband, a good enough man – good enough to take another's child as his own, and no ordinary child. Some folk said he was a changeling, with his black hair and black eyes and a way he had of looking at you. Others said he was an idiot child because he had not the power of speech. Whatever the truth of it, the sister and her man looked after him and brought him up with their own children.

'When the barons failed and Edward became King – ah yes, this is no ancient tale I tell you – the soldier's daughter took her husband and the boy and a little girl and boy baby no more than two years old and they found a safe place, well hidden from the King's anger. They lived a quiet life, as many did in those days. They had more babes. But the mother loved her sister's child above all the rest. And the changeling boy was no idiot. Far from it; he grew in learning. He learned from the working men; from the birds and beasts; he learned all the good brothers could teach him. He knew how to read the wind and the motion of the stars and how to speak to the wild creatures and how to physic. Above all, he loved music. One would think he had heard the stars sing while he was still in the womb.

'Then, one day, a stranger came to the village. He had heard tales of the marvellous boy who, some said, was wise as a heron though in speech he mumbled like an idiot. The stranger wanted to see for himself this changeling, this child of an English soldier's daughter and the Welsh lord that the stranger had served for many years. For when the lord lay dying he made his servant swear to find the boy, and bring him home to his family.

'The young man – for he was a young man by now – was drawn to the stranger by the power of music. And the stranger longed to take the young man back to his own folk in his own country but the time was out of tune – and the sharp-tongued sister sang her own discords! He had to return without the boy and wait for him to come of his own choosing. And so he did, with the help of the brother who was not his brother but who was as loyal and true as his mother, the plain, brown girl, the soldier's daughter with the sharp tongue – but the adventures of their coming are another tale. Not for today.'

The humming of the strings faded. Ieuan ap y Gof leaned forward and stared into our faces. 'Yes. That is the story. And if, in telling it, I chose wrongly, then so be it. But think of this: when you went to the holy well that night, you chose a time when you would meet with your kin, your *teulu*. The Lady Angharad was cousin to Meurig ap Dafydd, Ned's father.'

So many years ago. Time plays tricks with memory. Easy to look down the years and say Ieuan's story told me nothing I didn't already know. Oh, not the details, but always there was something different about the firstborn, and Mam's fierce love for him, this brother who was not my brother, and her never-ending cry: 'Look out for him!' What did it cost her to keep him? What did it cost her to let him go?

The boy looked back once. The girls were holding on to her skirt, the littlest one with her thumb stuffed in her mouth. Mam was staring after them, her face set like the skin on a two-day-old pudding. The boy didn't know whether she was more worried for herself and the lasses or for Ned. It wasn't for him. 'Look out for your brother'. It was almost the last thing she said to him but then, she'd been saying it all his life, ever since he could remember.

Twists and turns, twists and turns. I warned you. Remember? As many as the carvings of the old crosses. Or, as Ieuan said, like the serpent, looping around itself to bite its own tail. Listen – the bell for Vigils. Not for us – this night we keep our own watch and pray for all these souls.

'How did you hear about Ned?' Strange, that news of one village boy could travel across two lands.

'I would say chance, but is it ever so? A tale told one drunken night in the ale house and passed on – you know how it is. By your father, Will. He was goaded, it seems, by silly tongues clattering about his 'idiot boy' so he told more than he should. Praised Ned to the skies.' The music man laughed suddenly. 'He'd have made a good bard himself, from all accounts. He could have crafted a fine praise song. Your mother wasn't of the same mind, of course.'

Of course.

Brother John said he was a good father and a good husband and he deserved a place in heaven but Mam always said he was bound for hellfire. Mam never lied.

How did we feel, Ned and me, now we were no longer brothers? It was the same but not the same. We were still family but not the family bounded by father, mother, brothers, sisters. Like dropping a pebble into water, the ripples eddied larger and larger, further and further. Besides, we were bound by closer ties than blood; love and loyalty and danger shared and our lives held safe in the other's keeping. I think now, when Ieuan ap y Gof smiled to see us sitting close together on that infirmary bed, he knew the truth would bind us closer than ever, even as it parted us for ever.

Ieuan cradled the mended *crwth* on his lap as carefully as if it had been the hurt Llygad himself. 'My Lord Meurig offered this *crwth* as a prize, and Llygad won it in fair competition when he was still a young man. He had great skill. A *crwth* like this deserved a bard of great skill. It was made by a craftsman, a man with the eye of an artist. So fine, it needed no embellishment but see – silver tuning pins. And this – a silver tuning key bearing the initials of Meurig ap Dafydd.'

He held out the tuning key. Ned shrank back but I took it in my hand, wondering at its beauty. I turned it and its brightness caught in the firelight.

'Do you know how that was made, boys?'

I shook my head.

'First, a perfect model made from pale gold beeswax, with openings for molten metal to go in and out. The whole model was invested in special clay; completely enrobed, with great care and skill, before all was entrusted to a furnace, and heated until the clay was fired and the beeswax turned to liquid and the liquid to vapour that vanished like mist on a fine summer's morning. Lost wax – that is what this process is called. And the clay was now a mould waiting to be filled.

'The metal, the precious silver, was heated until it ran molten like moonlight and the craftsman tipped the liquid silver into the clay mould. He left it for an age until it was resolute. Then, carefully, carefully, he chipped away the clay to reveal the perfect version – the one you hold now in your hands.' He chuckled. 'I always think this was how God made us: the soft, perfect model that must melt and vanish before the precious metal can enter and the outer clay removed when its use is finished. Well, well. Llygad's *crwth* is a fine instrument; a prize worth the winning. Now he has returned it to me to give to his chosen successor, the son of Meurig ap Dafydd. Come, Ned: take it.'

He held out the *crwth*. Ned's body stiffened. He didn't move, and neither did Ieuan. He waited. Ned slowly, slowly uncoiled himself and moved to take the *crwth* from the music man. He stood there, hunch shouldered, as if he hardly knew what to do with it.

'Later, we shall write an elegy for my lord and lady so that they will always be remembered; now, it would be fitting if you played for us the Lady Angharad's song.'

Slowly, Ned lifted the leather strap and passed it about his neck. Slowly, he raised the *crwth* sideways to his body, as he had been taught. He took up the bow and the first notes breathed into the air.

He didn't sing, not this time, but still it was like a miracle: as if she herself were there in the room with us, her eyes clear as the windows in the brothers' great abbey, clear and luminous; eyes of doves by the rivers of waters; a lady of great goodness and beauty who lived again through music as surely as if Beuno himself had breathed life back into her. I swear the room was fragrant with the sweet smell of frankincense and violets.

✝ They did write an elegy. I heard it sung, not long after the end of the second war when I was in Wales searching for Ned and Ieuan. Without a doubt, it was their song – there was no mistaking the shaping of it.

A song I sang for Angharad before she died.
Gold girl, bright sun face, gift of goodness,
Gentle magnanimous girl
May she not want, may she find heaven…

Winter closed in. Sleet and snow fell and fettered our world. Night shadow cast gloom and storms howled. The life of the abbey went on, the bell calling the brothers to prayer at its set hours. This was a poor house, not like ours at home. There had been a fire some years before and new building was not yet finished. The church was simple, without even a cross shape. In spring, Brother Ifor said, building would start again. Maybe Ned and I could help? I was eager, ready to be doing something for these folk who had been so good to us. Now, in the winter months, when it was cold and dark came early, there was little to do outdoors but Ned and Ieuan kept strict hours of practice while I was given leave to look at the books that had been rescued from the fire, and those that were borrowed from greater abbeys.

'We have a book from our mother abbey,' said Brother Huw, 'from Longa Vallis – Abaty Cwm Hir.' He was not long since come from that place and was homesick for it, though he did not say so. I heard it in his voice. A green wilderness of high hills lay between that place and this. Cymer was lost in the folds of mountain and estuary, and it was poor. 'Look at this one.' The book was not huge, like the ones in our abbey, but it was beautiful; the Book of Genesis that told how mankind first lived in harmony with the rest of creation and then wilfully ruined it. Brother Huw was copying the script. It had taken much work and many hours and his sight was a fair way to being ruined. He showed me how he had rubbed the parchment with ground chalk to smooth it; how he had pricked the margins and ruled the lines ready for the text. I helped him mix black ink made from the gall wasp eggs laid in the soft twigs of oak trees. 'So many oak trees here. We are blessed,' he said in his lilting voice. He was a small, dark man of wiry build. He tilted his head on one side like a bird and, like a bird, he fluttered about his work. He said I had a steady hand, and he taught me to scribe; I longed to grind the pigments that made the colours: the blues and greens and vermilion and burnished gold leaf.

Later, when the snow had melted, we moved up to the abbey grange, high in the hills above the abbey. It was a remote place. 'Llewelyn stays here,' said Ieuan. 'It is safe here.' I wondered if we were hunted, even now, after the signing of the Treaty.

Spring came, and the woods and hillsides were alive with snowdrops and daffodils and celandines. From our nest high above the abbey we could see straight along the river to the sea. I stared at it for hour after hour. Some days it was hidden in mist. Other times it glittered and the horizon shimmered silver. Yet others, black storm clouds piled higher and higher and swept towards the land. Sometimes a ship steered across the horizon, sails shadowed against the light. I saw the sun sink into the sea, burning the sky red and orange and pink, and I thought about our own sea, where the sun rose out of it, soaking the land pale gold.

We went out with the lay brothers to tend the woodland. We were led there by a huge man they called Brother Cacamwri, though he had taken the name of Brother Eifion.

'A joke,' he said, 'because I am a tireless thresher. I am a great thresher. My father was before me, and his father before that. We have always worked on the land. There is an old story about a man called Cacamwri who threshed so hard with an iron flail that he tore the rafters of the barn to splinters.' He laughed: a big man's laugh.

There were great oaks here, broader than my arms could wrap round. There was one tree, already hollow, very old. If I had been younger, I would have played in its hollow. I was no longer young. Dic and his mates met us there. They were hard at work felling one of the oaks for the lord that owned land running alongside the abbey holdings.

'All the better for a wetting then, boys?' he said and laughed when we thanked him for saving our lives. It was all the same to him, filching what gold and lead he could find from the abbey mines or giving life back to two wretched boys drowning in the Mawddach falls. He'd a wife and two bairns, and a sweetheart in the next village; they were happy, so where was the wrong? Like Peter Long, I was thinking, though he seemed to belong to another life, lived long ago. I brought to my mind the day we had left Boston, sails slapping and snapping in the wind, and Peter's wench roaring into her apron and her belly swelled out like a wood pigeon stuffed full with food. Was she happy?

That was the day we saw the buzzard. The air was ringing with its cries. At first the sky was empty then there he was, riding the wind, wing tips tilted. I was thinking again about the scramble to the top of the old fort that morning, and looking out over the bright sea, and seeing life from high up, not like a worm. The pity I felt for the small things of this earth, the hunted things. The stoop of the buzzard: its keen claws, and death for the small things. Then I saw that the buzzard was hampered by crows. They wound round and round, up and up, forcing the buzzard higher and higher until he was lost to sight. Gone. No longer the attacker but driven away by black crows. I thought of his empty gut and his hunger. What was God's plan? Did he have one? Or was there nothing?

I was thinking then of Bogo. It was the first time I had let myself think of him, and his guts spilled out over the floor of the hall.

'Line up. Twos. Straighten up. Heads up. Chins up.'

'Try to look smart, you scum.'

'God save us, a fen fucking idiot.'

Bogo, bellowing.

In the first row to listen to the tale-telling.

A gash on his arm that was angry red: daring us to snigger.

'If I'd had a son like Dick, I'd have done the same.'

'Go, boy, go! Run!'

Bogo deserved an elegy, too.

One bright morning in March, Ieuan called us to him. 'See that mountain? Cadair Idris, it's called – the Chair of Idris. Whoever sleeps on the mountain through the night wakes a poet – or a madman. Let's see if the old tale holds true, hey boys?'

We climbed through the day; past the lake that was cradled in the shadow of the mountain, where we stopped and dabbled our feet in the spring chill. We climbed higher along a ridge and looked out over range after range of mountains, fading to blue mist. We climbed to the first peak. Because this is not a mountain that rises to one peak; there is a second peak, and it was here on the second that we made camp and lay down to sleep. But the wind howled and the stars were so bright they burned my eyes and I listened for Idris to climb out of his chair and find us; I was half frightened and half longing for him to touch me with his madness or his gift. And maybe he did.

April came. We went fishing in the nether fishery downstream from the abbey. When we came back, there was news of the October floods in the fens.

'Mam and the girls need me,' I said. 'They have no man.'

There was no choice. I had to go: Ned would stay where he belonged. After all, I had kept him safe and brought him home, though it was not the home he had left, and not his father's home. Lands, hall, all had been taken. Ned was the last of the family. He didn't care. He had the *crwth*. He was content to stay at the abbey with Ieuan, a *conversi* helping the brothers and making music. I gave thanks to Winifrede whose help I had begged, because he was truly home.

The day before I left I watched him and Ieuan walk through the orchard ahead of me. Clouds scudded and every apple tree was swilled with green and frothed with blossom and all the flowers of spring sprang up behind them where their footsteps trod; violets, celandine, primrose, daisies.

I wore clothes the brothers had given me but I had kept my pouch and now I felt the hard edges of something small and round in it. When I pulled them out, I saw yew berries, withered and wrinkled, from Winifrede's churchyard at Gwytherin. They spilled out of my hands and fell to the ground in the cloister walk. I like to think that near the wall of the abbey of Cymer grows this tree, Winifrede's yew, by God's grace.

The night before I left, Ned played for us. It was a new song, one he had made himself. It was the only other time I heard him sing, and it was for me; a praise song for the brother who was not his brother. And I wept.

There was no weeping after that. I left early on a bleak

morning of dismal rain. I was going downriver with the brothers, by boat to the grange at Neigwl in Llyn. From there I would take ship around the coast and up the Dee to Chester, past the new castles at Rhuddlan and Flint. As Ieuan said, new beginnings.

I walked away. I didn't turn round. I knew he was there on the path, hunched heron clutching the swan pipe to him, the short, round-shouldered man by his side, watching, watching, until I was long out of sight, disappeared into the rain clouds of the April morning.

Nine

All is duality. Man is finite and lives a finite time but the cosmos is unlimited, infinite. Odd and even; one and many; right and left; male and female; rest and motion; straight and curved; light and dark; good and bad; square and oblong: all exist and co-exist. From the Monad, the sanctified, comes unity. One and one creates the Dyad and mutability. Three is the beginning, middle and end. Four are the points that construct the pyramid, the sublime Tetractys. The unity of one becomes the unity of ten: the finite form emerges from the single, perfect point. Remember this.

I came back to the village early one May morning. The sun had risen, striking through the dew until the land steamed and my feet were lost in mist. As far as you could see was blue sky and white sheep on a green salt marsh where there'd been sea in winter. The air was full of the calls of water fowl and marsh bird and the hedge birds' twittering, warning cries. It sounded like home, and yet it was strange to me – or I was a stranger to it. It seemed I had been gone a long time but it was not even a twelve month since we had sailed from Boston.

Then, I was not yet eleven, and a boy: now, I was all but twelve, and a man. I'd heard on the road that the floods had hit Boston bad, but our village was safe. The sea banks had held along our stretch but all along its length they were making sure it was watertight for the autumn.

'A stitch in time,' one of them said.

'And, praise be to God, Edward's army is home to look after the land,' said the other. They looked at me curiously enough. 'D'you come from these parts?' they asked, but I told them nothing. I didn't see the need. I was no longer a mouth on legs, ready with a tale to tell. They would make their own stories without any help from me.

Hens were scratching in the dust and a cockerel crowed a warning. The village dogs stirred themselves, yapping and growling, but Ren, the oldest, remembered me and licked my hand. The rest clustered round her, cringing and pricking their ears all at the same time.

'Good girl. Where is everyone?'

A thin shape came into sight. I knew him at once.

'Will! Is it you? It's good to see you, boy. We've been that worried. We heard you'd gone missing. But you're alone – where is Ned?'

Alarm in his eyes. I shook my head. 'Safe, Walter. He stayed.'

Walter bent his head. He didn't look at me. His Adam's apple worked up and down, up and down. 'Did he find his music man after all?'

'Yes.'

He asked no more. Maybe he heard the stubbornness in my voice, or saw it in my eyes.

'You've grown, Will. Was it only a year ago?'

'Not even that. How is it here?'

It was then he told me about Gil Allbone. 'I think he was glad to go, Will, but his wife takes on. 'Appen she'll see it as a blessing before the year's out.'

Gil, Dick, John, dead; Ned left behind. Peter Long in the north with Godfrey Northumberland: Harold Edmundson who knew where.

'Ireland, they said. I don't know.'

I saw him, years later. Not Ireland, not then – Scotland it was. He'd married a lovely lass, a real Highlander, and they'd a brood of bairns. He spoke Gaelic better than he ever spoke English, for sure. It was the second time the Spotted Leopard was trying to take the land, and he went on trying until the day he died by the banks of the Solway. Hammer of the Scots, he called himself. Hammer of the Scots? He didn't ring true on the anvil. No sweet harmony from Edward. But that meeting with the Northman, yes, I remember that meeting well, very well. I'd reason to.

'There's just you and me, lad,' said Walter, 'and right glad I am to see you.'

'And Squire Phillip?'

'Aye, there's Squire Phillip an' all. He's the master now. His father took bad just before the floods. He died before the year was out.' Walter sucked his teeth. 'He's a good master, for all he's young. But we knew that already, didn't we, boy?'

No need to answer.

'Be sure to come by to see us, me and the missus. Best get to your mother and sisters now. They'll be glad of you, that's for sure.'

I wasn't so sure. Mam was alone, tending the fire and a pot of eels and the smell had me thinking of Peter Long. She stared at me, spoon in hand.

'Hello, Mam.'

Not a flicker of surprise or welcome.

'Best come in. You'll be hungry.' She gave the stew another stir. 'The girls will be glad to see you. They've been wondering.'

I could see she wouldn't ask. I said, 'He's safe, Mam. I took him home.'

Her shoulders slumped. I thought at first she was crying, but Mam never cried.

'That's all right then,' she said.

'He's with Ieuan.'

'Call the girls. We'll have a bite to eat and summat to sup.'

How could I tell her I knew it all? And where was the need? From that time on we never spoke a word about him, or what had happened. The only change was that she treated me like a grown man, the head of the household, and made sure the girls did the same.

Squire Phillip called. The girls were gawping and the littlest was sticking her thumb in her mouth and twisting her hair. Mam was that put out to have him in her cottage but proud. I'd lived long enough with Welshmen to know they bowed their head to no man so I spoke to him as one man does to another.

'You've grown a foot at least, Will. How's Ned?'

How, not where. He was a just man, and a fair one, so I told him.

'He'll be missed,' he said quietly. 'You'll miss him.' Then, 'They'll all be missed.' Eight from our village, and Squire Phillip made nine: three dead; three gone; three come back.

I stayed, of course. They needed me – not just Mam and the girls but the village. They needed men, and I wasn't a scrawny brat now but taller, broader, stronger, deft enough out on the marshes.

✝ Same, but not the same. Maybe I was the one who'd changed. The fens were flat. Oh, not just the flat of the land but dull, as if life and spirit had left. I missed the high places and the water falling like thunder headlong over rocks; I missed the sight of sea as blue as periwinkles – as blue as the eyes of the blacksmith's daughter met in another life.

I never saw her again – never saw Guillaume the Gascon who had been kind to me on the march to Chester. I heard he lived and went home to the woman who was his wife and the boy about my age. He was sure to take Ned's pipe of elder, and tell the tale of how he came by it. I like to think Guillaume's son got a sound – a tune, even – or a sound like a fart that made him giggle.

I wonder where he is now, the man who was a boy about my age.

Well, you know what happened: Dafydd's wild attack on Hawarden and Wales in flames; Llewelyn murdered, and his men slaughtered; the land laid waste. Dafydd betrayed and taken. His was a savage death, savage, and the man who carried out the gruesome task was paid his twenty pieces of silver. The *Croes Nawdd* was stolen from the country. Edward was no fool;

he brought it back to England. They say he melted down the royal seals of Gwynedd and turned them into a chalice for the monastery at Vale Royale. A poisoned chalice, if you ask me.

At home, we had the great flood and Mam and the girls dead. My eldest sister was nine months gone and the baby all but born. Ralf's coming, and Ned's swan pipe. I have it by me still – and I learned to play it. But not like Ned. Never like Ned.

It was after the great flood that I chose to go from this flat land that dulls the mind, back to the mountains and the rushing waters of Wales. I wanted to find Ned. I knew now I should never have left him. Like the monks of Bardney, I had made the wrong choice; I'd shut out the saint and I had lost my soul.

I couldn't find him, or the music man. No one had news of them. There was a new abbot at Cymer and no word of Abbot Llewelyn, alive or dead. The land was a lost place, destroyed by war and hopelessness, and it was only folk like old Derw who kept faith. And his was a strange faith, when all was said and done.

I went from place to place, country to country, searching, telling my stories to those who chose to listen. But why tell you what you know? Except for this.

One night I was in the lowlands of Scotland. It was that time when late summer becomes early autumn. There was a full moon, a huge, red moon that looked close enough to touch. Baleful, it seemed to me. Edward's army was there, and I was the entertainment. A man has to earn a living. No harm in that. Besides, I gleaned what news I could and carried it across to the Scots. I saw two men I knew: one in the front row, knife out, whittling at a wooden pike head; the other a pale ghost in the shadows. Twenty years on and I knew them at once. Who could mistake?

I told the tale of Winifrede, and how her uncle, the great Beuno, breathed life into her head and she lived. I told a story of betrayal, of innocent blood spilt, of my lord and my lady and the bairn and their kin. And Bogo, the life giver, helping two boys escape into the night. And how a great music man breathed life into the *crwth* and sang of the dead lady's goodness and beauty, and how she lived, like the firmament, unchanging for ever.

As I told the tale, I watched the faces of the two men I knew.

Next morning, one was dead, stabbed through his black bull's heart by a man who looked like a ghost, with white hair and lashes and pale blue eyes and pale skin and who never quite spoke our tongue, though he knew the Gaelic.

I kept on travelling. Rome, Jerusalem, Santiago de Compostella – I'm three times a pilgrim, three times blessed! I heard of Edward's death and his wish – leopard to the last – to have his bones, those long shanks, boiled from his body so they could be carried into battle. Well, everyone knows that didn't happen. He was buried, all pomp, in a blue robe crammed with gaudy glass jewels. Maybe time will tell what he meant by it.

So I stayed away, always searching for news of Ned and Ieuan, but there were only ever rumours, never quite real. It was as if they had gone into the ether, into the firmament itself. I wasn't always alone – don't think that. There were women. Some for pleasure, that's true, but others because we shared our souls. I remember – well, never mind, that's all gone now. For all I know, I've a brat or two in this world. They've never seen fit to find me. Better not, maybe. I'd not have been much of a father, that's for sure. I'd got the taste for travelling, and the traveller's life. And the women? Ah, a storyteller's life is a lonely one. Best lived alone.

Then there was news of Edward's son, that peacock, the 'Welsh prince' he'd promised us, born in Caernarfon, the show place, as gaudy as the glass jewels on his shroud. I've seen it. Built with stones taken from the old Roman town – it's a wonder he didn't call himself Macsen Wledig and have done with it. But he was Edward II, who was murdered. A red-hot poker, they said, shoved where it well belonged, up his arse to hurry him to hell.

And Gwenllian: Llewelyn's daughter, the last of the line of Gwynedd. She'd been brought here to the flat lands far from her home – and did she ever know who she was, the babe who was taken and bound in the nunnery at Sempringham for ever and ever, until death? There were those who knew but it would have been death to speak out.

She's been dead these six months past, you say?

Her cousin Gwladys, Dafydd's daughter, died in the convent at Sixhills not more than a year ago. Did you know that?

Oh, the children, the children. Edward was a cruel man. Dafydd's boys, close confined in Bristol castle, one starved to death, the other a mouse in a cage for year after weary year until the world forgot he had ever existed. And the other girls – what happened to them? Not a word, not a rumour.

I came back home – not home, though I call it so. It suits

me well enough. It's comfort you want when your bones ache and your sight's failing. No, never a word of Ned or Ieuan ap y Gof. I have heard the nine orders of the angelic choirs in the corners of the earth, and I have suffered the nine orders of devils in the rings of hell, but I never found them. Who knows what happened to them? They had lives enough, like cats, but I think now they are in the illimitable, immutable, infinite world beyond this. I listen and listen but I cannot hear their music.

Though last night…last night, I wondered if I heard the swan pipe. Fleeting notes, sweet as only Ned could play them. But no. It was the sound of the wind in the reeds. That was all. Yes, that was all.

Come now; it's late. The fire's dying and it's time you were abed. The bell will call for Lauds before you've had a wink of sleep. You must be tired, listening to an old man's ramblings. It was all so long ago.

Ten

x

x x

x x x

x x x x

Huddle into yourself. Heft the blanket round you. Ice cracks in its folds, settles into silence. Frost ghosts the marsh grass. Nightjars are noiseless. Dark rises up from the land. It swallows the sky. No moon: it is neap tide. The sea is hussing behind the sea bank, safe, caged. Wind shivers hard reeds. They rattle like bones. Far off, a screech owl on the hunt. Black pools glitter with stars. The real stars are high above. They are singing inaudibly, endlessly, in the cosmos that stretches to infinity over the flat fens. Tonight, if you listen hard. Tonight, if you are patient. Huddle inside your whitening shroud. Settle yourself to wait.

Acknowledgements

For their help, patience and encouragement.

The staff of Haverfordwest Library; Bob Evans and Mary-Anne Roberts of 'Bragod'; Nigel Jenkins; Dr Paul Wright of Trinity University College, Carmarthen; Albie Smosarski; my sons, of course; all those people met briefly who gladly shared information and expertise, particularly Dai Morgan Evans.

Further reading from Honno

The War Before Mine, by Caroline Ross
A brief wartime romance leaves Rosie heartbroken and pregnant, not knowing if Philip – on a suicide mission designed to stop the Nazi invasion – is alive or dead. "More than a war story, more than a love story... A slice of living history." Philip Gross.
978 1870206 97 6
£6.99

About Elin, by Jackie Davies
Elin Pritchard, ex-firebrand, is back home for her brother's funeral. Returning brings all sorts of emotions to the fore, memories good and bad, her own and those of the community she left behind.
978 1870206 89 1
£6.99

Hector's Talent for Miracles, by Kitty Sewell
Mair's search for her lost grandfather takes her from a dull veterinary surgery in Cardiff to the heat and passion of Spain. "An intelligent and sympathetic exploration of the lasting damage done to survivors of war" Planet
978 1870206 81 5
£6.99

Girl on the Edge by Rachel V Knox
A chilling story of love, betrayal, secrets and lies… Just how did her mother die and what did Leila witness on the cliff

top, if anything? A compelling psychological thriller set in the moors of North Wales.
978 1870206 75 4
£6.99

Death Studies, by Lindsay Ashford
Some secrets haunt the living and the dead... A windswept seaside strip in West Wales – sleepy enough, until three bodies turn up within as many days. A shocking coincidence or a serial killer? The third title in the Megan Rhys crime series.
978 1 870206 86 0
£6.99

Other titles in the Megan Rhys Crime series, by Lindsay Ashford

Frozen, by Lindsay Ashford
Two young prostitutes have been murdered but there is something wrong with the information the police are giving Megan. The first title in the Megan Rhys crime series from Lindsay Ashford. "Gritty, streetwise and raw" Denise Hamilton, author of the Eve Diamond crime novels
978 1 870206 82 2
£6.99

Strange Blood, by Lindsay Ashford
Women are dying with pentagrams carved on their faces. Satanic ritual or cunning deception? Second title in the Megan Rhys crime thriller series. Shortlisted for the

Theakston's Old Peculier Crime Novel of the Year, 2005.
978 1 870206 84 6
£6.99

The Killer Inside, by Lindsay Ashford
When the predators become the prey, not even prison bars will keep them safe. The fourth title in the Megan Rhys crime thriller series
978 1 870206 92 1
£6.99

Honno Classics

Iron and Gold, by Hilda Vaughan
A skilful retelling of the best known Welsh Fairy Bride folktale, 'The Lady of Llyn y Fan Fach'.
978 1870206 50 1
£8.99

Strike for a Kingdom, by Menna Gallie
The secrets and tensions of a close-knit mining community are exposed in the reprint of this 'outstanding detective story', set at the time of the miners' strike in 1926.
978 1870206 58 7
£6.99

Betsy Cadwaladyr: A Balaclava Nurse - An Autobiography of Elizabeth Davis
A republication of the fascinating story of the nineteenth century Welsh woman Elizabeth Davis, also known as Betsy

Cadwaladyr, the 'Balaclava nurse'.
978 1870206 91 4
£8.99

Queen of the Rushes, by Allen Raine
First published in 1906, a masterful novel and an enthralling tale of the complex lives and loves, set at the time of the 1904 Revival.
978 1870206 29 7
£7.95

Dew on the Grass, by Eiluned Lewis
An enchanting autobiographical novel set in the Welsh borders, a must for anyone studying 1930s literature.
978 1870206 80 8
£8.99